NEW YORK REVIEW BOOKS
CLASSICS

PARTY GOING

HENRY GREEN (1905–1973) was the pen name of Henry
Vincent Yorke. Born near Tewkesbury in Gloucestershire,
England, he was educated at Eton and Oxford and went on
to become the managing director of his family's engineering
business, writing novels in his spare time. His first novel,
Blindness (1926), was written while he was at Oxford. He
married in 1929 and had one son, and during the Second
World War served in the Auxiliary Fire Service. Between
1926 and 1952 he wrote nine novels—*Blindness, Living, Party
Going, Caught, Loving, Back, Concluding, Nothing,* and
Doting—and a memoir, *Pack My Bag.*

AMIT CHAUDHURI is Professor of Contemporary
Literature at the University of East Anglia. He has written
several works of fiction, a critical study of the poetry of D. H.
Lawrence, and edited *The Vintage Book of Modern Indian
Literature.* Among the many awards he has received are the
Commonwealth Writers' Prize, the Los Angeles Times Book
Prize for Fiction, and the Government of India's Sahitya
Akademi Award. He is a Fellow of the Royal Society of
Literature, and is also a musician.

BY HENRY GREEN
(published by NYRB unless otherwise noted)

Back
Introduction by Deborah Eisenberg

Blindness
Introduction by Daniel Mendelsohn

Caught
Introduction by James Wood

Concluding (forthcoming from New Directions)

Doting (forthcoming)
Introduction by Michael Gorra

Living
Introduction by Adam Thirlwell

Loving
Introduction by Roxana Robinson

Nothing (forthcoming)
Introduction by Francine Prose

Pack My Bag (published by New Directions)

Surviving: The Uncollected Writings of Henry Green (forthcoming)
Introduction by John Updike

PARTY GOING

HENRY GREEN

Introduction by
AMIT CHAUDHURI

NEW YORK REVIEW BOOKS

New York

THIS IS A NEW YORK REVIEW BOOK
PUBLISHED BY THE NEW YORK REVIEW OF BOOKS
435 Hudson Street, New York, NY 10014
www.nyrb.com

First published in Great Britain in 1939 by the Hogarth Press.

Library of Congress Cataloging-in-Publication Data
Names: Green, Henry, 1905–1973, author. | Chaudhuri, Amit, 1962– writer of
   introduction.
Title: Party going / Henry Green ; introduction by Amit Chaudhuri.
Description: New York : New York Review Books, [2017] | Series: NYRB
   Classics
Identifiers: LCCN 2016026858 | ISBN 9781681370705 (softcover : acid-free
   paper) | ISBN 9781681370712 (epub)
Subjects: LCSH: Rich people—England—Fiction. | Upper class—England—
   Fiction. | Social classes—England—Fiction. | England—Social life and
   customs—20th century—Fiction. | BISAC: FICTION / Psychological. |
   FICTION / Satire. | FICTION / Literary. | GSAFD: Satire.
Classification: LCC PR6013.R416 P37 2017 | DDC 823/.912—dc23
LC record available at https://lccn.loc.gov/2016026858

ISBN 978-1-68137-070-5
Available as an electronic book; ISBN 978-1-68137-071-2

Printed in the United States of America on acid-free paper.
10 9 8 7 6 5 4 3 2

INTRODUCTION

IN THE late 1980s, when I was a graduate student in Oxford, I
bought a compendious volume. I don't like big books, but this volume included three novels. They were by an author I hadn't heard of,
Henry Green. The Green whom people were talking about then had
an *e* at the end of his surname, and his first name was Graham. He
was almost an exact contemporary of Henry's: born in 1904, a year
before Green, he lived much longer. Both belonged to well-to-do
families, but Green was particularly affluent. His father was an in-
dustrialist. I'd tried reading Graham Greene, because I liked the titles of his novels and because everyone who read novels seemed to
have read him, but had never made much headway, presumably because of my inability to focus on narrative fiction. Then Henry
Green came along, and Graham swiftly became, for me, the "other
Greene," and then not even that. Although relatively few people
had, or have, read Henry Green, there's an irreducible, longstanding
excitement about him among those who have, an excitement that
makes him periodically palpable to us. On the other hand, English
novelists who were famous in their day—Graham Greene, but also
Angus Wilson and Iris Murdoch—are now either largely forgotten
or have turned into minor literary historical facts. Time is noncha-
lant in its workings, but Green is exceptionally stubborn, and is still
among us.

I must have bought the three-novel volume of *Loving*, *Living*, and
Party Going because John Updike had, in his introduction, not only
given Green centrality as a precursor, but called him a "saint of the
mundane." The religious analogy was excessive and pseudo-Joycean,

but what had made me admire Updike in the first place, in *Rabbit, Run* and some of the stories about the town of Tarbox and the fractious, self-indulgent couple the Maples, was the way in which he'd deliberately made room for the mundane, for the banality that constantly fills our lives and makes them truly interesting. And yet I found Green to be a different kind of writer from Updike, with almost none of the chronicler's impulse that from time to time directed the latter's decade-long projects, and with no abiding interest in realism, despite his extraordinary eye and ear and his gift for capturing character. Replying to a question put to him by Terry Southern for *The Paris Review* in 1958—"You've described your novels as 'nonrepresentational.' I wonder if you'd mind defining that term?"— Green said:

> "Nonrepresentational" was meant to represent a picture which was not a photograph, nor a painting on a photograph, nor, in dialogue, a tape recording. For instance, the very deaf, as I am, hear the most astounding things all round them which have not in fact been said. This enlivens my replies until, through mishearing, a new level of communication is reached. My characters misunderstand each other more than people do in real life, yet they do so less than I. Thus, when writing, I "represent" very closely what I see (and I'm not seeing so well now) and what I hear (which is little) but I say it is "nonrepresentational" because it is not necessarily what others see and hear.

Green in fact stands somewhere between James Joyce, in his tendency to be intolerant of "normal" English syntax and punctuation, and Virginia Woolf, in his sense of how narrative can be shaped by things outside of event. But, as is clear from his remarks to Southern, he further conflates his aesthetic with disability and eccentricity. (Right at the start of the interview, he refuses to field an inconvenient question on the grounds that he can't hear the interviewer, though it quickly becomes evident that the deafness is opportunistic.) More than Joyce and Woolf or any other writer I can think of,

Green's contribution to the modern novel is the imprimatur of an unapologetic eccentricity and, through it, a reconfiguring of the idea of singularity.

I have seen that Picador omnibus edition in the hands of readers and teachers, creased, carried with a degree of protectiveness. But, by all accounts, it didn't do well and soon went out of print. Since then, Green's nine novels have had spasmodic resurrections, come and gone and come back again. What will it take for Green to penetrate the general consciousness? His writing went out of view after he died in 1973 (and he hadn't written a book for twenty years before that), though more recently a handful of influential literary champions made him something of a cause. But maybe it's to do with what Ezra Pound called "the age." Maybe the recent decades haven't been receptive to a novelist whose sole purpose seems to be to fashion a language with which to communicate joy and delight. Woolf was shockingly neglected; her present status is owed not so much to literary critics as it is to feminism. Jean Rhys was utterly forgotten until her last work, *Wide Sargasso Sea*, allowed her to be annexed later by postcolonialists, who focused on its Creole rewriting of Charlotte Brontë. Joyce's mythic scaffolding and verbal play identified him to academia as being essential both to modernism and to the project of hermeneutics. I mention these writers not only because of their capacity to transform and delight but also because some aspect of their writing has been translated advantageously into a set of terms that are important to particular literary historical moments. With Green, we're presented with a singular kind of artist who, like the poets of ancient India and Greece, has nothing to offer us but delight. We don't know what to do with such a writer.

I hesitate to call *Party Going* a modernist work because it's sui generis, stands on its own, and has not lent itself out to the modernism industry. But it has something in common with standard modernist texts, by which I mean not only what Frank Kermode called its mythic structure, or its mythic punctuation of dead pigeons and bathing women, or its purgatorial fog-bound environment, or the occasional abnormality of its syntax, but the fact that it's interested in not the journey but the waiting, not the event but the interruption. Dense fog in London causes all trains to be canceled. Traffic on the roads is at a standstill; some of the people on their way to the station have to abandon their cars and walk—a moment of both liberation from, and loss of, class privilege. Among throngs of frustrated but jubilant commuters a group of rich people has convened; they expect to travel to the south of France as guests of the rich and intoxicatingly eligible Max Adey. Two women especially are in pursuit of Max: Julia Wray and Amabel. Max has been meaning to escape Amabel and make this trip with his friends and acquaintances, but she tracks him down. In the meantime, through the good offices of Julia's uncle, a very important person in the railways, the whole group has been moved to the station hotel and given rooms with baths. An old aunt has fallen ill after picking up and washing a dead pigeon, and seems to be on her deathbed in a hotel room. The shutters to the station have been brought down to keep more people from getting in. Amabel somehow finds her way inside despite these impediments, and Max is at once ashamed, caught out, and temporarily disarmed by her immense beauty. It seems to Julia, whom Max had been courting in a room not long ago, that her romantic holiday with Max—though she would disdain to think of it in those terms— is not to be.

The simultaneity of the narrative makes it less like a text overseen by an omniscient narrator than a particular kind of cinema, a cinema not so much invested in a single protagonist as in what's happening at once in several rooms and the spaces around them. Not Christopher Isherwood's camera, then, which records in Berlin the dissolution of ways of life with faux objectivity and a doomed helplessness, but multiple cameras at work. The material has been organized by an auteur akin, in his method, to a film editor, as a montage of swiftly juxtaposed scenes that creates an illusion of unity and continuity. The film I have in mind is Jean Renoir's *The Rules of the Game*, which is about a group of upper-class people with conflicting love interests who find themselves stranded along with their servants in a manor house on a country estate during the weekend. The restricted but unique locale and the limited duration of the action allow Renoir to explore how people, animals, and objects might inadvertently *make* a narrative out of nothing. The director observes not so much the characters and their surroundings (he does this, of course) as the patterns out of which this narrative is produced. *The Rules of the Game*, released like *Party Going* in 1939, isn't about either belonging somewhere or being in exile; it is about inhabiting a transient, busy state of unfinishedness. The aesthetic of the two works is remarkably congruent. Both also appear just prior to the destruction of the worlds contained within them, and both possess an odd indestructibility. Renoir's film was trashed by both the right and the left for its pointless portrayal of the wasteful rich. It was taken off screens prematurely and then banned, only to be recognized in later decades as a landmark of cinema.

Another film comes to mind, by Satyajit Ray, Renoir's most gifted student. From 1962, *Kanchenjungha* is Ray's first film in color, and the first he scripted himself. It's named after the mountain peak that the upper-class holiday-makers in the film are from time to time reminded of as they mill around the hill station of Darjeeling: they believe a glimpse of the mountain would make their excursion worthwhile. They are completely self-absorbed, while Kanchenjungha offers an opening into a world beyond that refuses to present itself, though these people themselves are in fact already in the open, as they explore, or loiter, in Darjeeling's narrow lanes and inclines. "Can you believe this place was nothing but a Lepcha village before the British turned it into this town?" says the insufferable patriarch Sir Indranath towards the end of the film. Empire! It was insubstantial by 1962, like the mist. It's becoming intangible in *Party Going* too, but not quite as much. It's there, in the global allusions, in the great railways.

Ray's film is in real time. The experience of reading *Party Going* approximates this—the sense of having entered, via the sentence, a specific continuum and time span. The four or five hours it takes to finish the novel is also the period in which the fog rolls in and then starts to lift. The spell lifts too, and, like Rabindranath Tagore after he finishes reading Kalidasa's *Meghdoot*, we realize we've entered a world we can't possess. (Tagore records his experience of temporarily inhabiting the world described in the long fourth-century Sanskrit poem in his own 1889 poem of the same name.) This conflation of the characters' time with the reader's (embedded in which is the nine years it took for Green to write the book) points to the author's preoccupation with, and mastery of, form, which is another kind of reality from the one the novel is depicting—the consequence of his abstract "nonrepresentational" method.

One looks to other genres and art forms for analogies because *Party Going* isn't a novel in the usual sense of the term. It gives us a wonderfully comic account of its characters, but it is also an assemblage—of moments, and of different kinds of awareness of the world and even of writing. Green is nothing if not conscious of his literary context: when Julia walks to the station and registers the procession of headlights in the dark, the narrator points sideways to the novel's antecedents: "These lights would come like thoughts in darkness, in a stream...." Then there are the epic similes, more reminiscent of Kalidasa and classical Sanskrit poetry and Indian iconography than Homer and even Milton, and signaling to us that Green lived in a time when the English writer's inheritance went far beyond European modernism. Here the narrator describes two people in Max's party waiting in the station to spot their host:

> Like two lilies in a pond, romantically part of it but infinitely remote, surrounded, supported, floating in it if you will, but projected by being different on to another plane, though there was so much water you could not see these flowers or were liable to miss them, stood Miss Crevy and her young man, apparently serene, envied for their obviously easy circumstances and Angela coveted for her looks by all those water beetles if you like, by those people standing round.

This is almost outrageous, except that Green makes these semi-ironical, vivid comparisons repeatedly. On the next page, the simile concerns the station master's view of crowds of smokers, "every third person smoking it might all have looked to Mr. Roberts, ensconced in his office away above, like November sun striking through mist rising off water." As Max and Amabel talk to each other on the phone before he heads off to the station (he is lying to her about his intentions), her observation that "here we are like a couple of old washerwomen slanging away at each other" sounds more striking than it should, as if Amabel were unwittingly situating the story in a world history of the epic. Two pages on, as Alex proceeds down the dark, fogbound street in a taxi, it seems that the "[s]treets he went through were wet as though that fog twenty foot up had deposited water, and reflections which lights slapped over the roadways suggested to him he might be a Zulu, in the Zulu's hell of ice, seated in his taxi in the part of Umslopogaas with his axe, skin beating over the hole in his temple...."

And Robert Hignam, as he presses through the crowd in the station, remembers:

> When small he had found patches of bamboo in his parents' garden and it was his romance at that time to force through them; they grew so thick you could not see what temple might lie in ruins just beyond. It was so now, these bodies so thick they might have been a store of tailors' dummies, water heated. They were so stiff they might as well have been soft, swollen bamboos in groves only because he had once pushed through these, damp and warm.

The shutters are soon going to come down in the station, keeping new commuters out; Max's group is going to be at once nervously and luxuriously ensconced in the station hotel. Despite the sense of enclosure and imprisonment ("we are simply in a state of siege you know, yes, no one's allowed in or out. Yes, nanny and her friend are with us, they have been angels"), the narrative has already ramified and been placed in the "world": *Party Going* is both a comedy and a cosmology. It's not about being hemmed in or trapped, or about being English. It enacts a fluidity of perception where it's also about being Zulu, about people being compared to branches, to "household servants in a prince's service," where Amabel is known not only in London but in "Northern England" and Hyderabad, where the "thousands of Smiths, thousands of Alberts, hundreds of Marys" seen gathered below from a hotel window seem "woven tight as any office carpet or, more elegantly made, the holy Kaaba soon to set out for Mecca." *Party Going* is partly art-house movie, with a unique soundtrack, and partly one of those extraordinary British texts, like *Briggflatts* or *The Anathemata*, in which locality, eccentricity, and even class flow in and out of other cultures. It's this flow that is envisaged here in terms of the din, the murmurs, the silences, the laughter, and the courtships that occur while the trains have stopped, so that any moment things might open up in an unlikely way, as in this passage about Max falling asleep briefly in a room in the station hotel with Amabel in his arms, whom he will unexpectedly lose interest in upon waking up: "It was so luxurious he nodded, perhaps it was also what she had put on her hair, very likely it may have been her sleep reaching out over him, but anyway he felt so right he slipped into it too and dropped off on those outspread wings into her sleep with his, like two soft evenings meeting."

—AMIT CHAUDHURI

PARTY GOING

FOG WAS so dense, bird that had been disturbed went flat into a balustrade and slowly fell, dead, at her feet.

There it lay and Miss Fellowes looked up to where that pall of fog was twenty foot above and out of which it had fallen, turning over once. She bent down and took a wing then entered a tunnel in front of her, and this had DEPARTURES lit up over it, carrying her dead pigeon.

No one paid attention, all were intent and everyone hurried, nobody looked back. Her dead pigeon then lay sideways, wings outspread as she held it, its dead head down towards the ground. She turned and she went back to where it had fallen and again looked up to where it must have died for it was still warm and, everything unexplained, she turned once more into the tunnel back to the station.

She thought it must be dirty with all that fog and wondered if it might not be, now it was dead, that it had fleas and they would come out on the feathers of its head but she did not like to look as there might have been blood. She remembered she had seen that with rabbits' ears when they had been shot and she remembered that swallows were most verminous of all birds—how could it have died she wondered and then decided that it must be washed.

As Miss Fellowes penetrated through at leisure and at last stepped out under a huge vault of glass—and here people hurriedly crossed her path and shuttled past on either side—Miss Crevy and her young man drove up outside and getting out were at once part of all that movement. And this affected them, for if they also had to engage in one of those tunnels to get to where they were going it was not for them simply to pick up dead birds and then wander through slowly. Miss Crevy had hat-boxes and bags and if her young man was only there to see her off and hate her for going and if Miss Fellowes had no more to do than kiss her niece and wave good-bye, Miss Angela Crevy must find porters and connect with Evelyn Henderson, who was also going and who had all the tickets.

People were gathering everywhere then at this time and making their way to the station.

Of their party two more had also arrived who like Miss Fellowes had only come to wave good-bye; two nannies dressed in granite with black straw hats and white hair. They were just now going downstairs in the centre of an open space and those stairs had LADIES lit up over them.

Meantime Miss Crevy's young man said:

"This porter here says the fog outside is appalling, Angela darling." He went on to say it was common knowledge with all the porters that no more trains would go out that evening, it was four-thirty now, it would soon be dark, then so much worse. But she said now they had got a porter it would be silly to go away and certainly she must see the others first. Besides she knew Robin did not want her to go and though she did not mind she wondered how much he wanted her to stay. Anyway, nothing on earth would prevent her going. Their porter then made difficulties and did not want to come with them; he would only offer to put her things in the cloakroom, so her young man, Robin, had to tip him in advance and so at last they too went in under into one of those tunnels.

Descending underground, down fifty steps, these two nannies saw beneath them a quarter-opened door and beyond, in electric light, another old woman who must be the guardian of this place; it might have been one of their sisters, looking upstairs at them. As they came down she looked over behind her and then back at them.

For Miss Fellowes, as they soon saw, had drawn up her sleeves and on the now dirty water with a thin wreath or two of blood, feathers puffed up and its head sideways, drowned along one wing, lay her dead pigeon. Air just above it was dizzy with a little steam, for she was doing what she felt must be done with hot water, turning her fingers to the colour of its legs and blood.

No word passed. The attendant watched the two nannies who stood in a corner. In one hand she gripped her Lysol bottle, her other was in her pocket and held a two-shilling piece that Miss Fellowes had slipped her. She whispered to them:

"She won't be long," and turning she watched her stairs again, uneasy lest there should be more witnesses.

At this moment Mr. Wray was telling how his niece Miss Julia Wray and party would be travelling by the boat train and "Roberts," he said over the telephone, "get on to the station master's office, will you, and tell him to look out for her." Mr. Wray was a director of the line. Mr. Roberts said they would be delighted to look out for Miss Wray and that they were only too glad to be of service to Mr. Wray at any time. Mr. Wray said "So that's all right then," and rang off just when Mr. Roberts was going on to explain how thick the fog was, not down to the ground right here but two miles out it was as bad as any could remember: "impenetrable, Mr. Wray—why he must have hung up on me."

"What I want now is some brown paper and a piece of string," Miss Fellowes quite firmly said and all that attendant could get out was, "Well, I never did." Not so loud though that Miss Fellowes could hear; it was on account of those two nannies that she minded, not realizing that they knew Miss Fellowes, sister to one of their employers. They did not say anything to this. They did not care to retire as that might seem as if they were embarrassed by what they were seeing, speak they could not as they had not been spoken to, nor could they pass remarks with this attendant out of loyalty to homes they were pensioners of and of which Miss Fellowes was a part.

And as Miss Fellowes considered it was a private act she was performing and thought it was a bore their being there, for she saw who they were, when she went out she ignored them and it was not their place to look up at her.

Now Miss Fellowes did not feel well, so, when she got to the top of those steps she rested there leaning on a handrail. Miss Crevy and her young man came by, Miss Fellowes saw them and they saw her, they hesitated and then greeted each other, Miss Crevy being extremely sweet. So was she going on this trip, too, Miss Fellowes asked, wondering if she were going to faint after all, and Miss Crevy said she was and had Miss Fellowes met Mr. Robin Adams? Miss Fellowes said which was the platform, did she know, on which Miss Crevy's young man broke in with "I shouldn't bother about that, there'll be no train for hours with this fog."

"Then aren't you going with them all?" and saying this she took an extra grip on that handrail and said to herself that it was coming over her now and when it did come would she fall over backwards and down those stairs and she smiled vaguely over clenched teeth. "O what a pity," she said. Below those two nannies poked out their heads together to see if all was clear but when they saw her still there they withdrew. And now Miss Crevy was telling her who was coming with them. "The Hignams," she pronounced Hinnem, "Robert and your niece Claire, Evelyn Henderson, who has all our tickets, Julia, Alex Alexander and Max Adey."

"Is that the young man I hear so much about nowadays?" she said and then felt worse. She felt that if she were going to faint then she would not do it in front of this rude young man and in despair she turned to him and said: "I wonder if you would mind throwing this parcel away in the first wastepaper basket." He took it and went off. She felt better at once, it began to go off and relief came over her in a glow following out her weakness.

"Do you mean Max?" Miss Crevy asked self-consciously.

"Yes, he goes about a great deal, doesn't he?"

She was reviving and her eyes moved away from a fixed spot just beyond Miss Crevy and, taking in what was round about, spotted Mr. Adams coming back.

"How kind of him," she said and to herself she thought how wonderful it's gone, I feel quite strong again, what an awful day it's been and how idiotic to be here. "Then you won't be even numbers, dear, will you?"

"No, you see no one quite knew whether Max would come or not."

As she had not thanked him yet Adams thought he would try to get something out of this old woman, so he said:

"I put your parcel away for you."

"Oh, did you find somewhere to put it, how very kind of you. I wonder if you would show me which one you put it in," and when he had shown her she made excuses and broke away, asking Miss Crevy to tell Julia she would be on the platform later. Once free of them she went to where he had shown her and, partly because she felt so much better now, she retrieved her dead pigeon done up in brown paper.

The main office district of London centred round this station and now innumerable people, male and female, after thinking about getting home, were yawning, stretching, having another look at their clocks, putting files away and closing books, some were signing their last letters almost without reading what they had dictated and licking the flaps where earlier on they would have wetted their fingers and taken time.

Now they came out in ones and threes and now a flood was coming out and spreading into streets round; but while traffic might be going in any direction there was no one on foot who was not making his way home and that meant for most by way of the station.

As pavements swelled out under this dark flood so that if you had been ensconced in that pall of fog looking down below at twenty foot deep of night illuminated by street lamps, these crowded pavements would have looked to you as if for all the world they might have been conduits.

While these others walked all in one direction, the traffic was motionless for long and then longer periods. Fog was down to ground level outside London, no cars could penetrate there so that if you had been seven thousand feet up and could have seen through you would have been amused at blocked main roads in solid lines and, on the pavements within two miles of this station, crawling worms on either side.

In ones and threes they came into the station by way of those tunnels, then out under that huge vault of glass. As they filed in, Miss Fellowes, who was looking round for a porter to ask him which platform was hers, thought every porter had deserted. But as it happened what few there were had been obscured.

At this moment Mr. Roberts, ensconced in his office where he could see hundreds below, for his windows overlooked the station, was telephoning for police reinforcements. "There are hundreds here now, Mr. Clarke," he said, "in another quarter of an hour these hundreds will be thousands. They tell me no buses are running and 'this must be one of those nights you'll be glad you live over your work,'" he said. Then they talked for some time about who was to pay for all this—as railways have to keep their own police—and they enjoyed quoting Acts of Parliament to each other.

One then of legion when she had left her uncle's house, Miss Julia Wray left where she lived saying she would rather walk. With all this fog she felt certain she would get to the station before her luggage.

As she stepped out into this darkness of fog above and left warm rooms with bells and servants and her uncle who was one of Mr. Roberts' directors—a rich important man—she lost her name and was all at once anonymous; if it had not been for her rich coat she might have been any typist making her way home.

Or she might have been a poisoner, anything. Few people passed her and they did not look up, as if they also were guilty. As each and every one went about their business they were divided by this gloom and were nervous, and as she herself turned into the Green Park it was so dim she was sorry she had not gone by car.

Air she breathed was harsh, and here where there were no lamps or what few there were shone at greater distances, it was like night with fog as a ceiling shutting out the sky, lying below tops of trees.

Where hundreds of thousands she could not see were now going home, their day done, she was only starting out and there was this difference that where she had been nervous of her journey and of starting, so that she had said she would rather go on foot to the station to walk it off, she was frightened now. As a path she was following turned this way and that round bushes and shrubs that hid from her what she would find she felt she would next come upon this fog dropped suddenly down to the ground, when she would be lost.

Then at another turn she was on more open ground. Headlights of cars above turning into a road as they swept round hooting swept their light above where she walked, illuminating lower branches of trees. As she hurried she started at each blaring horn and each time she would look up to make sure that noise heralded a light and then was reassured to see leaves brilliantly green veined like marble with wet dirt and these veins reflecting each light back for a moment then it would be gone out beyond her and then was altogether gone and there was another.

These lights would come like thoughts in darkness, in a stream; a flash and then each was away. Looking round, and she was always glancing back, she would now and then see loving couples dimly two by two; in flashes their faces and anything white in their clothes picked up what light was at moments reflected down on them.

What a fuss and trouble it had been, and how terrible it all was she thought of Max, and then it was a stretch of water she was going by and lights still curved overhead as drivers sounded horns and birds, deceived by darkness, woken by these lights, stirred in their sleep, mesmerized in darkness.

It was so wrong, so unfair of Max not to say whether he was really coming, not to be in when she rang up, leaving that man of his, Edwards, to say he had gone out, leaving it like that to the last so that none of them knew if he was going to come or not. She imagined she met him now on this path looking particularly dark and how she would stop him and ask him why he was here, why wasn't he at the station? He would only ask her what she was doing herself. Then she would not be able to tell him she was frightened because he would think it silly. She would hardly admit to herself that she was only walking to try and calm herself, she was so certain he would not come after all.

It was so strange and dreadful to be walking here in darkness when it was only half-past four, so unlucky they had ever discussed all going off together though he had been the first to suggest it. How did people manage when they said they would do something and then did not do it? How silly she had been ever to say she would be of this party for now she would have to go with them, she could not go home now she was packed, they would not understand. But how could people be vague about going abroad what with passports and travelling? He had her at a hopeless disadvantage, he could gad about London with her gone and go to bed with every girl.

She realized that she was quite alone, no cars were passing and by the faint glow of a lamp she was near she could see no lovers, even, under trees.

It came to her then that she might not have packed her charms, that her maid had left them out and this would explain why things were so wrong. There they were, she could see them, on the table by her bed, her egg with the elephants in it, her wooden pistol and her little painted top. She could not remember them being put in. She turned round, facing the other way. She looked in her bag though she never carried them there. It would be hopeless to go without them, she must hurry back. Oh why had she not gone in the taxi with her things?

And as she turned back Thomson went by with her luggage, light from his taxi curving over her head. She did not know, and he did not know she was there, he was taken up in his mind with how difficult it was going to be for him to find Miss Henderson and how most likely he would miss his tea.

Meantime, as he was letting himself into his flat, Max was wondering if he would go after all. It would mean leaving Amabel. Blinds were drawn, there was a fire. He could not leave Amabel. Edwards, his manservant, came in to say that Mrs. Hignam had rung up and would he please ring her back. He did not like to leave Amabel. He asked Edwards if his things were packed and he was told they nearly were. Well if his bags were ready then he might as well leave Amabel.

Julia, crossing a footbridge, was so struck by misery she had to stand still, and she looked down at stagnant water beneath. Then three seagulls flew through that span on which she stood and that is what had happened one of the times she first met him, doves had flown under a bridge where she had been standing when she had stayed away last summer. She thought those gulls were for the sea they were to cross that evening.

Mr. and Mrs. Hignam were on their way, crawling along, continually in traffic blocks so that their driver was always folding his arms over the wheel and resting his head.

Claire Hignam was talking hard and fast. First she told her husband Robert she had rung Max up to say they were just off and to ask him why he was not already on his way. He had told her he was not packed yet but she had known enough of him not to believe that. Edwards was too good a servant to leave things so late and anyway Max could not give straight answers.

"D'you suppose we shall see Nannie on the platform, it's so touching really how she always comes to see me off."

As he did not reply she went on to ask him if he had seen that Edward Cumberland was dead, so young. He paid no attention for he was thinking of something he had forgotten. She explained she had been in too much of a rush to tell him before and he then said tell him what? At this she said he was maddening, didn't he realize this boy had died when he was only twenty-six? He said what of? She did not know and what on earth did it matter anyway, wasn't the awful thing that he was dead and at twenty-six? She went on that she would live till she was eighty-four. He made no answer. Then she said this dead man was a cousin of Embassy Richard's, what did he know about that?

(It appears that a young fellow, Richard Cumberland, was so fond of going out that, like many others, he often went to parties uninvited. A Foreign Embassy was entertaining its Prince who was paying visits in this country and someone had stolen some sheets of Cumberland's note-paper and had sent to every newspaper in London asking them to put the following in their Court Columns: Mr. Richard Cumberland regrets that he was unavoidably prevented by indisposition from accepting His Excellency the Ambassador's invitation to meet his Prince Royal. This notice had duly appeared and the Ambassador, thinking to strike out for a host's right to have what guests he chose, had written to the Press pointing out that he had never invited Mr. Cumberland and that this gentleman was unknown to him. The whole subject was now being discussed at length everywhere and in two solicitors' offices and in correspondence columns in the Press.)

He could not tell her anything that she did not already know but he thought perhaps they might hear some news when they got to the station.

"If we ever get there," she said. "Really it is too awful trying to get round London nowadays. We've been fifteen minutes already, block after block like this it's too frightful."

Even then she had no train fever, she was confident their train would not go without her. But Miss Evelyn Henderson, who had been urging her driver on and telling him every moment of short cuts to take which he knew would delay them, was in a great rush and bother when she was driven up. Fumbling to pay him off in her bag bulging with the others' tickets she told her porter they were certain to be separated, they must meet where luggage was registered, under the clock. He said which one, there were three. Under the clock she said and then they were gone.

Inside, dolled up in his top hat, the station master came out under that huge vault of green he called his roof, smelled fog which disabled all his trains, looked about at fog-coloured people, his travellers who scurried though now and again they stood swaying and he thought that the air, his atmosphere, was wonderfully clear considering, although everyone did seem smudged by fog. And how was he going to find Miss Julia Wray he asked, whom he did not know by sight, and when by rights he should be in his office.

Miss Fellowes also considered how she was to find her niece. She did feel better but not yet altogether safe, if her faintness had left her she was not confident it would not return. She decided that it would be better for her to sit down.

Those two nannies were already over cups of tea when they saw her come in and look round for somewhere to sit. She saw an oval counter behind which two sweating females served and round it, one row deep, were chromium-painted stools, like chrysanthemums with chromium-plated stalks. Each one of these was occupied but there were some other seats of canvas with chromium plate again so that, associating them with deck chairs, for an instant she indulged herself with plans of sea voyages and the South of France. All these were also taken except one and on this she sat down, holding her dead pigeon wrapped up on her lap and waiting to be served.

As time went by and no one came to take her order she knew how tired she was. Although this was her first time out today she thought she might have been through long illnesses she felt so weak. She saw there was only one waitress to serve customers beyond that counter and as she was still waiting she understood at last that it was for her to fetch what she wanted. Leaving the pigeon in her place, and asking a man next her to keep it, she went to see.

At first all those two nannies noticed was that Miss Fellowes had gone up to the counter and they did not doubt but what she was ordering tea. They were not surprised when she was not served as they themselves had been kept waiting. But as they watched her they soon saw that thin-lipped flush which, with their experience, told them that for Miss Fellowes all this was getting past all bearing. They knew what it meant and they could have warned her it was useless to give girls like these a chance to answer back. You had to be thankful if you were served and it only made things worse to complain as she was doing.

Then they realized that words were passing, but what shocked them most, when it was over and Miss Fellowes was walking back to her seat, was to see that it was not tea she had ordered, what she was carrying back was whisky. They were sorry to see her order and sorry again for all this had drawn attention to her. One rough-looking customer in particular eyed her rather close.

Miss Fellowes did not care, she could dismiss things of that kind from her mind and entirely ignore at will anything unpleasant or what she called rude behaviour, so long as this was from servants. It had been a fancy to order whisky and she was trying to remember what her father's brand had been called which was always laid out for them years ago when they got back from hunting. He said it was good for everyone after a hard day and you drank it, went to have your bath and then sat down to high tea. And now how extraordinary she should be here, drinking in tea rooms with all these extraordinary looking people. And there was that poor bird. One had seen so many killed out shooting, but any dead animal shocked one in London, even birds, though of course they had easy living in towns. She remembered how her father had shot his dog when she was small and how much they had cried. There was that poor boy Cumberland, his uncle had been one of her dancing partners, what had he died of so young? One did not seem to expect it when one was cooped up in London and then to fall like that dead at her feet. It did seem only a pious thing to pick it up, though it was going to be a nuisance even now it was wrapped up in paper. But she had been right she felt, she could not have left it there and besides someone might have stepped on it and that would have been disgusting. She was glad she had washed it.

The man who had eyed her, spoke.

"Them girls is terrible I reckon," he said. "Trouble enough many of us 'ave had to get here without they refuse to serve you."

"Yes," she said, "it's quite all right now, thank you," and hoped he was not going to be a nuisance. She wondered whether she had been wise to choose spirits, she really did not feel well, they did not seem to have done her any good.

Meantime Claire and Evelyn had met and were greeting each other in the Hall for registering luggage with cries not unlike more seagulls. Robert was taking off his hat and saying, "Why hullo Evelyna," and she was asking them where everyone was and telling them she had seen Thomson with Julia's luggage who said Julia had started out on foot, could anyone imagine anything so like her? Where on earth was Angela, or Max and Alex? Did anyone know if Max meant to come? Claire said she had telephoned and that she thought he would. "Anyway," said Evelyn, "I've got their tickets here. Now Robert, you and Thomson had better go and try and find them all, will you please at once? Thomson go with Mr. Hignam and see if you can bring Miss Crevy and the others back here will you? You haven't seen anything of Edwards I suppose? No, then just do that, will you Robert, we must be all together. Now dear," she said turning to Claire, "we can sit on our things and have a good chat." They then sat down on their luggage to discuss indifferent subjects very calmly while porters, leaning on their upended barrows, went to sleep standing up. So calm was Evelyna she made one wonder if, now those two men had gone, she was not more at ease.

They had been addressed in much the same tone of voice as if both had been in service and Robert Hignam remarked to Thomson that it looked like the hell of a job this time. "It's not going to be easy." "No sir, it's not," and on that they separated and were at once engulfed in swarming ponds of humanity most of them at this particular spot gazing at a vast board with DEPARTURES OF TRAINS lit up over it. This showed no train due to leave after half past two, or two hours earlier, or, in other words, confusion.

Miss Crevy and her young man were standing in the main crowd. She was very pretty and dressed well, her hands were ridiculously white and her face had an expression so bland, so magnificently untouched and calm she might never have been more than amused and as though nothing had ever been more than tiresome. His expression was of intolerance.

Like two lilies in a pond, romantically part of it but infinitely remote, surrounded, supported, floating in it if you will, but projected by being different on to another plane, though there was so much water you could not see these flowers or were liable to miss them, stood Miss Crevy and her young man, apparently serene, envied for their obviously easy circumstances and Angela coveted for her looks by all those water beetles if you like, by those people standing round.

Surrounded as they were on every side yet they talked so loud they might have been alone.

"Well, whatever you say I must go and find the others."

"But Angela, I've told you it can't be done in this crowd."

"I know you have, but how else am I going to get my tickets?"

"What d'you want tickets for now? I tell you they'll never get trains out of here."

"But Robin, it's been paid for. And I want to go, don't you see."

At this someone pushed by them, saying he was sorry and that finished it.

"Well," he said, "I must go, good-bye, enjoy yourself," and then it was all so unjust he added, although it made him feel a fool, "I don't ever want to see you again." She kissed him on his nose as he was turning away, conscious that she was behaving well, and then he was gone.

If that swarm of people could be likened to a pond for her lily then you could not see her like, and certainly not her kind, anywhere about her, nor was her likeness mirrored in their faces. Electric lights had been lit by now, fog still came in by the open end of this station, below that vast green vault of glass roof with every third person smoking it might all have looked to Mr. Roberts, ensconced in his office away above, like November sun striking through mist rising off water.

Mostly dressed in dark clothes, women in low green or mustard colours, their faces were pale and showed, when not too tired, a sort of desperate good humour. There was almost no noise and yet, if you were to make yourself heard, it was necessary to speak up, you found so many people were talking. Having never been so surrounded before, and with what was before her, she felt excited. She felt she must get to the side and was surprised to find she had been in quite a small crowd for here almost at once were fewer people.

Coming up to her the station master asked if she could by any chance be Miss Julia Wray, and, taken aback, she could only say no, she had not seen her. As he passed majestically on, murmuring regrets, she wondered whether she ought not to run after him to say she was in her party, but then that seemed absurd, Julia was sure to be where their luggage was to be registered, she could tell her then.

And as Miss Crevy made her way to this place, Claire and Evelyna had arrived at that stage in their conversation when they were discussing what clothes they were bringing. Both exclaimed aloud at the beauty and appropriateness of the other's choice, but it was as though two old men were swapping jokes, they did not listen to each other they were so anxious to explain. Already both had been made to regret they had left such and such a dress behind and it was because he felt it impossible to leave things as they were with Angela, it was too ludicrous that she should go off on that note, that kiss on his nose, he must explain, that Robin came back to apologize.

He found her quite soon and not so far away. She did not seem surprised at his turning up again and told him about the station master. He did not see what this had to do with it and plunged into how sorry he was, he had had an awful time coming up with her again, would she forgive him? He thought what had done it was her ancient friend giving him that parcel to get rid of and then, as soon as he had carried that out, sending him to get it back for her. This made Angela quite cross, she told him he had been very rude, and that he had better stay away if he was going to be tiresome.

Julia had been back to her room and had not found her charms. It had been bare as though she had never lived there. Her curtains were down, they were being sent to be cleaned, her mattress had gone and her pillow cases were humps under dustsheets in the middle of her bed. Thinking it unlucky to stay and see more and besides Jemima swore that everything was packed in the cabin trunk, she called them her toys, Julia had fled by taxi this time.

Feeling rather faint she hurried through tunnels, made her way dazedly through crowds which she only noticed, to ask herself what she would do if she could not find the others and was surprised to find Claire and Evelyn where they were sitting on their luggage.

She asked how were they, darlings, and they asked her, and they kissed and all sat down again. She wanted to know where everyone had got to and saw poor Evelyna was in a great fuss which made her

feel calmer in that she now felt resigned. And indeed Evelyn considered that she must do something, she told herself that if she did not
deal with this situation they would be sitting here till domesday and
that without her not one of this party would catch their train. So she
said it must be a waste of time to try and register luggage with all the
piles of it waiting in front of theirs, and she would try to find out
something about their train. With that she was gone.

Used to having everything done for them, Julia and Claire settled
down to wait. Soon Julia asked if Claire had seen Max and was told
about their telephone conversation. She tried to make out whether
this had been before she had imagined meeting him in the Green
Park and took some comfort from deciding that it must have been.
But she did not feel reassured. She tried to discuss how other travellers were dressed, where they could be seen at intervals standing
about, many of them almost hidden by their luggage. She never mentioned Max. There was a silence and at last she coughed and said:

"Really he's hopeless, isn't he, don't you think?"

Max was still in his flat. He was also drinking whisky and soda. His
arm-chair was covered with thick fake Spanish brocade, all the coverings were of this material with walls to match, fake Spanish tables
with ironwork, silver ashtrays, everything heavy and thick, all of it
fake, although he thought it genuine, and it was expensive in pro-
portion. That is to say that if all these things had been authentic he
would not have had to pay more, anyone less well off could have
bought museum pieces cheaper.

He answered the telephone after he had let it ring for some time.
Amabel said:

"Is that you, Max?"

"Who is it speaking?"

"Oh, Max, are you really going?"

"Why?" said he.

"I mean must you really go?"

"Just hang on a moment will you, there's something here," and he put the receiver by and taking his glass he shot his whisky and soda into the fire. It went up in steam with a hiss. He stood still for twenty seconds then he went and mixed himself another. When he came back to the telephone she said:

"Have you got someone else there?"

"No. Why?"

"I thought I heard you shushing someone. What were you doing then?"

"I was putting water on the fire, soda water if you want to know."

"People don't put soda water on fires."

"I did. My paper caught alight and I had to put it out."

"Max, I must see you. Supposing I came round now if I promised to be good."

"What?"

"I said I could come round now if I swore to you I wouldn't be silly? Oh, Max."

"But what is it about?"

"I won't have you go, that's all. I can't bear it."

"I didn't say I was going."

"It's unfair, we've had such a marvellous time together, I do love you so, darling love. Why can't we be as we were? I swear to you I won't be tiresome again. You must believe me, darling."

"I rang you up yesterday."

"Did you?"

"You weren't in."

"I expect I was having my hair done. I was there all afternoon. Max, who have you got with you, I heard them whispering just now?"

"And what were you at last night?"

"What was I at? How can you say things like that? Max, darling, what has come over you lately?"

"I rang up about half past nine."

"I was lying down, you know all this has made me quite ill and I had such a business getting on to Dr. Godley, his line was engaged all the time, I expect I was ringing him up."

"I didn't get the engaged signal."

"Max, my darling, I shan't argue, you have only to ask Marjorie, she was with me later. I wish you would get on to her, my dear, she could tell you the state she found me in. She was horrified."

"I'm sorry."

"Max, my darling, I'm so bewildered and miserable I really don't know where I am. What has happened to make everything different, it was all so perfect before and now here we are like a couple of old washerwomen slanging away at each other whenever we meet? Darling, really the whole thing is making me ill. Dr. Godley says the best thing for me to do would be to go away to the sun out of this frightful fog for a month or two to give my system time to right itself. He says my whole system is out of gear and wants toning up."

"Well, look here, are you doing anything this evening?"

And as she was saying no she was not, Edwards, his manservant, came in to say his bags were packed.

"Just a moment, Am," he said. "What's that?"

"Your bags are all ready, sir."

"Who was that, darling?"

"It's only Edwards asking if I wanted any tea."

"Ask him from me if his little boy is any better, will you?"

"I will."

"What were you going to say?"

"Look here, supposing you came round about half past nine, we could go out and have dinner somewhere."

"Oh, darling, that would be perfect, you are an angel, so you are not going after all?"

He said, "That's settled then," and rang off.

"Is the car round?"

"Yes, sir."

"My bags in? Yes, then come on, I'm in a hurry." Edwards put on a black bowler hat, Max had no hat at all and he drove his rich car off at speed.

He drove hard, by back streets to avoid traffic blocks, swinging his big car round corners too sharp for it and driving too fast. Edwards said it was bad weather for getting about in, was there not one air service operating and he said no, and there wouldn't be today of all days.

"I doubt if your boat train will run, sir."

"That's not the point, I've got to go."

So what made him drive faster, and taxi drivers and others drew up their cars and shouted after him, was that he felt he was treating her badly. If he must get away then it was not right to leave her by asking her round to find him gone. He was sick and tired of it. All the same it was bad to ask her round to find he'd gone, that was all there was to it.

Accordingly when they drew up at the station, where at once a little crowd collected to admire his car, he put it to himself that what he wanted was a drink, so he told Edwards to get his luggage registered, Miss Henderson would have the tickets, and that he would be along later. Then he went in under into a larger tunnel that had HOTEL ENTRANCE lit up over it.

He engaged a sitting-room which had a bedroom off, for when he told them what he wanted they explained they had no sitting-rooms without bedrooms and that he would have to engage both. This was typical of his whole style of living, he was always being sold more than he need buy and he did not question prices. Once in this room, with his drink ordered, he rang up Amabel. His trouble was inexperience, he could not let good lies stand.

"Why, darling, it's you again," she said.

"About this evening. Look here, don't come after all."

"Whyever not?"

"It won't be any good."

"But you said I might."

"I shan't be there."

As she did not reply, he said he could not be there.

"You mean to tell me you are going after all?"

"Yes, I'm at the Airport now," he said, and because she must not find him here, she would make a scene, he rang off before she had found anything to say. He gave up his room at once.

Meantime Alexander was on his way, bowling along in his taxi the length of cricket pitches at a time, from block to block, one red light to another, or shimmering policemen dressed in rubber. Humming, he likened what he saw to being dead and thought of himself as a ghost driving through streets of the living, this darkness or that veil between him and what he saw a difference between being alive and death. Streets he went through were wet as though that fog twenty foot up had deposited water, and reflections which lights slapped over the roadways suggested to him he might be a Zulu, in the Zulu's hell of ice, seated in his taxi in the part of Umslopogaas with his axe, skin beating over the hole in his temple, on his way to see She, or better still Leo.

He did not know where he was, it was impossible to recognize streets, fog at moments collapsed on traffic from its ceiling. One moment you were in dirty cotton wool saturated with iced water and then out of it into ravines of cold sweating granite with cave-dwellers' windows and entrances—some of which he began to feel he had seen before till he realized he was in Max's street.

He thought he had told his driver to go to the station but when they drew up outside Max's block of flats he realized he must have given this address, probably because he had been wondering if Max had really meant to come. He was then all at once completely given over to train fever, his driver did not know what time it was, he rushed into the lift, rang Max's bell, asked Franklin what time it was, found Max had already gone and that it was much later than he thought, ran downstairs because he thought it would be quicker, and, lying back panting, trembling, said to his driver,

"Hurry, hurry."

"Where to?"

"To the station of course."

"Which station?"

"For France, stupid."

As he climbed into his cab his driver said:

"Another bloody one of those."

All this time Julia and Claire had been sitting by their trunks.

They had not spoken of Max again, and this is where Edwards came upon them as he followed Max's luggage. Julia sprang up.

"Oh, Edwards, there you are," she said. "Where is Mr. Adey?"

"I couldn't say, Miss."

"Didn't he come with you?"

"Yes, Miss."

(Edwards had learned never to give information about his gentleman to ladies.)

"Then isn't he in the station?"

"I couldn't say, Miss."

Claire then took her turn, "Where did he go when he left you?" she asked him.

"He told me to meet him here, Madam."

Both girls, as though by consent, dropped it and left well alone. It had come to both of them that where he was now of course was in the lavatory.

Alex drove up, still haunted by how late he was. Getting out he screamed for porters and, when he found one, he told him they must meet again at the registration place, he had no time, he must fly and he rushed off, forgetting to pay his taxi. The driver was at once hysterically angry, called out warnings to everyone near about Alex, said to that porter, "Wait for me, mate," drove his taxi nine feet forward to where he thought it would cause more obstruction, said, "Where's a bloody copper?" and with Alex's luggage, and his porter, also went in under into one of those tunnels and was gone.

So now at last all of this party is in one place, and, even if they have not yet all of them come across each other, their baggage is collected in the Registration Hall. Where, earlier, hundreds had made their way to this station thousands were coming in now, it was the end of a day for them, the beginning of a time for our party.

Anyone who found herself alone with Julia could not help feeling they had been left in charge. Again there was so much luggage round about in piles like an exaggerated grave yard, with the owners of it and their porters like mourners with the undertakers' men, and so much agitation on one hand with subdued respectful indifference on the other that this uneasiness had at last been passed on to Claire. Several other passengers were nearly in hysterics. And as she was used to leaving all her worries to her husband, who had to do everything for her, this was one of those moments when she missed him. She felt almost cross with Julia for being so helpless.

She said to Julia there did not seem to be much point in waiting for Evelyn to come back, they might try to get some of their luggage registered now, it would be such a rush when they did begin with all the mountains of stuff already waiting. Looking up from where she sat she put this to her porter drooping over his barrow. He told her nothing was being accepted for registration on account of there being no trains running as she could see for herself; he seemed pleased, he spat, and then became more despondent.

When once she had put her anxiety into words it was as though she had screamed after having tried not to for some time, when in pain. She might easily have got into the state that woman was in there, whose hat had all but fallen over her face, when she saw Alex waving, waving and smiling to them while making his way. He kissed them both while she was still saying "why, here's Alex." He asked where was Max, not here he supposed, and they said of course not. Claire explained how appalling it was they would not register any luggage, but already her fears had left her and she was joking and he laughed and said they never would if they could possibly avoid it, and they all laughed, too, and spoke at once. "Anyway," he said, "they can't surely expect us to sleep here."

"Alex darling, what is it about this fog, there isn't any where we are, isn't it rather tiresome of them?"

"They say it's down to the ground outside London, you see, Julia, and they can't get through, why, I can't imagine."

"But do you think they're really doing anything about it?"

He said they must be and then described his adventures while on his way to them. They laughed again. Then he asked if they had heard the latest about Embassy Richard, he had been told the postmark on that letter was St John's Wood, which must mean Charlie Troupe had sent it. Claire said that if he meant the letter enclosing his advertisement for *The Times* then she had heard from someone in that office there had been no postmark at all, it had come unstamped. Alex said that if it did not have a stamp then it would have had one of those things which show you what you have to pay, and that must have been postmarked. Usually anything that had not been stamped was covered with postmarks, and even times of posting, and they rang your bell to tell you. "It's rather like travelling on trains," he said, "without your ticket. They make you pay and write you out one, putting down where you got on and where you are going to." Claire said yes, but you could not ask letters where they had been posted, and so this argument might have gone on if Miss Henderson had not returned. She was quite sure any unstamped letter would have two postmarks.

Edwards asked Julia, who had not been paying attention, what was to be done about all this luggage. She said she did not know and wasn't it awful. "You'd better ask Miss Henderson, she has just been to try and find out."

Now what Evelyn Henderson had in mind was this: she had most of their party in one place and it would be best to keep them here until all were assembled whatever their chances of getting a train later. She was not sure any trains would run ever again, but if she had said she was going and had closed up her flat then she would make every effort to get away. She was afraid some of them might go home and leave it for her to ring them all up if there was any chance of their getting off and that would mean muddles and incompetence and end by their not going at all. So she said:

"It can't be Charlie Troupe, the thing's absurd, he'd never do anything like that, he's an old friend of mine. About this beastly train I can't imagine why they are keeping us here like sheep in a market. An inspector was very nice and told me that the fog was lifting outside, so I don't suppose it will be too long now."

"But, darling, in that case don't you think we ought to try and find Max at once?"

"I know, Julia, but Robert and Thomson have gone to look for him."

"No, that's just it, they're hunting round for Angela. Don't you think we ought to send Edwards after him?"

Alex announced he could see Angela and then that she could see him. "Can't you find her, there, behind that fat man, look she's waving, who's the individual with her?"

The individual with Miss Angela Crevy was her young man, Mr. Robin Adams, who so objected to her going away with them, he hated them so much.

"There they all are," Angela said to him, "except I don't see Max."

Yes, Mr. Adams thought to himself, that was like Max, the offensive swine, it was like him not to turn up when this was his party so to speak, as he would be paying for them. It went against the grain to have men of his type paying for Angela. It was not her fault, she did not realize, but when she had been about a bit more she would be sorry she hadn't taken it in.

For a moment Mr. Adams even felt jealous of Alex.

They had drawn nearer, they were all now waving to each other, or rather Angela was waving to them and they were all waving back. Looking at them Mr. Adams thought what a bloody lot of swine they were. His one consolation was that he expected a most frightful display of affection when they were within speaking distance. He was not disappointed. Alex's voice came to them, high-pitched:

"Have you brought your bed with you, darling? I can't remember whether I told Mr. Crump to pack mine, because we'll never get away from here," and he added with intuition, "Evelyna won't let us."

Angela replied, "but darling, didn't you pack a double bed for us then?" Her young man asked himself what could be in worse taste and then was heartened when he saw how badly they had taken it. Of course she did not know them well enough to say things of that kind he thought, and he was wrong. In their day they had made too many jokes in that strain, they were no longer amused, so they took it just as he had done for a different reason.

They were shaking hands and Angela told Claire she had seen her aunt, "ages ago back there among all those people. I can't tell you what a time we've had trying to get to you, didn't we, Robin? It's such an enormous place, we couldn't find where to go and I got into such a fuss."

A faint sound of cheering came from right away at the back of this station. Heads turned towards it and Julia could see a waiter who was looking out of one of the hotel windows and who seemed to be miles away, he looked so puny, joined by another at this window and both leaned out to watch something below them.

"What can it be?" she said under her breath, "I do feel so nervous."

She thought here was their party laughing and shrieking as though nobody was going travelling; and then no one but her seemed to mind where Max was; where could her charms be? Jemima said she had put them in the cabin trunk but she would look in her dressing case, they were more likely to be there.

Squatting down apart she opened this case. Everything was packed in different coloured tissue papers. They were her summer things and as she lifted and recognized them she called to mind where she had last worn each one with Max. She often went away weekends to house parties and it often happened that he was there. If she had no memory for words she could always tell what she had worn each time she met him. Turning over her clothes as they had been packed she was turning over days.

Her porter sighed. He had enjoyed what he had seen of her things.

Thinking she might have been upset by their talk of Embassy Richard and because he liked to sympathize, Alex came up and asked if she was sick to death of their discussing that silly business and postmarks and all that. He found, as he had not realized, there was so much noise she could not hear what he said. Or perhaps she was crying. Julia still kept her head turned so he could not see but when he repeated himself she said yes, it was ridiculous wasn't it? He craned round and saw she was not crying and then she knew he was looking for tears.

"Oh dear," she said, "there are so many—too many people, aren't there?"

Alex told her he thought there would soon be many more and that he found it bewildering.

So did Mr. Hignam, pushing his way through crowds, only his word for it was appalling. He felt probably they had already found Angela for themselves, there ought to be dogs, he thought, to find people for them. Though he would be sorry for dogs in this crowd, it was a wretched business, damp and cold, everyone looked as if they had had enough. How anyone was going to get a train was obviously more than the railway people could imagine. He found himself by a bar and that was an idea. They could not expect you for ever to go round shouting Angela where are you? It was crowded but he would fight through and have one.

Max was already drinking in this bar. After ringing up Amabel he had wondered if it would not be possible for her to trace where he was through the Exchange, so he had paid his bill and left. Then he had not felt up to meeting the others yet, and in any case he did not mind where they were. His feeling was he must get across the Channel and it was better to go with people than alone.

Forcing his way through, meeting half resistance everywhere and that hot smell of tea, cups guarded by elbows and half-turned bodies with "mind my tea," Robert thrust on and on. When small he had found patches of bamboo in his parents' garden and it was his romance at that time to force through them; they grew so thick you could not see what temple might lie in ruins just beyond. It was so now, these bodies so thick they might have been a store of tailors' dummies, water heated. They were so stiff they might as well have been soft, swollen bamboos in groves only because he had once pushed through these, damp and warm.

His ruined temple then appeared, still keeping to whisky, seated on one of those chrysanthemums with chromium-plated stalks which Miss Fellowes had observed. And she was still here, not feeling so well again, all of her turned in on herself, thrusting her load of darkness.

Robert was not so pleased to see Max, but both were polite

enough to say hullo. Robert asked him if he had seen Claire's aunt by chance. Max did not hear, so let it pass. Robert asked again, this time he put it this way, that Claire had sent him to find her aunt. There was too much noise, it did not reach Max. He shouted back, "what will you have?"

"I've ordered, thanks."

"I suppose they sent you to find me," Max said and now that he had begun to talk it seemed easier to hear. Robert answered no, it was Claire's aunt who was lost. Oh, said Max, and was she coming too, and once again Robert thought how odd he was, it was practically his party and yet he did not seem to know who would be coming and appeared to be quite ready to have Claire's aunt along, although they meant to be away three weeks. He explained that she had only come to see them off. "Don't know the party," Max said.

Robert told him all the others were waiting by their luggage until such time as it could be registered and Max asked where Edwards was. Max then said perhaps they had both of them better get back to the girls. Robert told him he thought there was no hurry, no trains were running yet.

"I know, old boy, but we can't leave your wife and the girls on their own like that."

"Well, Edwards is there and they've got their porters, they'll be all right."

"They'll be all right of course, but what we don't want them to do is to go back home, we must get off to-day."

Again Robert thought it was unlike Max to say that. No one had been sure that he would even get to the station and yet here he was anxious they should all go with him.

"Let's keep them waiting once in a way," Robert said, "and anyway I can't go back without finding her. Have you seen Alex? I was to find him too." And then it struck him he had never been sent to find Claire's aunt, Evelyn had wanted him to get hold of Alex and Angela and Max, but she had said nothing about Miss Fellowes. Why then had he been looking for the aunt? At that moment he saw Miss Fellowes.

"But, good God, Max, there she is." Max did not seem to hear and he was pleased, it would have been too difficult to explain.

"And, my God, there's Claire's nannie."

"Have another, Robert?"

"No, thanks. I say Max, the old girl doesn't look any too good, does she?"

"I haven't made her out yet. Well, now you've found her we can get along."

"You don't understand, I wasn't sent to find her, but I don't like the way she looks, old boy. Do you see her there?"

"Do you mean that woman with the parcel?"

"Yes, holding the whisky. Look here, Max, she's sitting all on a skew."

"Why not go up and ask her."

"I can't. I say, would you mind just keeping an eye on her and I'll be off and bring Claire along?"

Max agreed and ordered another drink. Both had forgotten the nannies who sat anxiously by in silence. And that man, who had spoken to Miss Fellowes earlier, kept his attention on her, one or two others watched and each time this man looked away from her he winked.

As Hignam made his way back Alexander's taxi driver arrived. He came up to Alex and said "how now." Then he described what streets they had been through on their way and what his clock showed when he had left his cab. He said it was larceny to bilk taxi drivers. Alex asked how he could think he was trying to get away without paying, no trains could or would leave that evening or afternoon and anyway, he had paid, he said. His porter was brought in to witness, he had seen no money pass, Alex's voice became more shrill. Evelyn said it did seem ridiculous to be expected to pay twice when taxis were now 9d for the first mile. Then Julia stopped it by saying all this was more than she could stand and begged Alex not to be difficult. His answer was to move with the taxi driver out of earshot, where they went on gesticulating, though it was obvious now that they were suddenly on the best of terms.

"It did seem so silly, didn't it?" Julia said. "Don't you think, darlings?"

"Oh, I don't know, poor Alex, but they seem to be getting on very well together now," said Evelyna, and then went on "here's Robert coming, Claire."

"Well," said his wife, as he came up, bullying him at once, "I suppose you didn't find them. Angela's been here for ages, and so has Alex."

"I say, Claire, a most extraordinary thing happened," Robert said and drew her aside. "You know I went to find Alex and Max as you told me. I got to the bar and thought I would go in and have a drink. Well, I found Max in there having one too and the next thing I did was to ask him if he had seen your aunt."

"But you idiotic old thing, that wasn't what you were sent to do. Nobody mentioned her."

"Yes, you did, Claire. But wait a moment. The odd thing was that just after I'd asked Max about her I actually did see her there."

"I don't see anything funny in it at all. You never could keep anything in your head. But you found Max anyway, although you don't seem to have been looking for him. Why are you always like this? Yesterday I asked you to put more coal on the fire and you passed me the egg."

Robert thought no one would ever understand, it had been a shock to him, his mind had been full of the others and then he had blurted her name out and on that had seen her sitting there. Perhaps there was nothing in it but he wondered.

"Look here, she did not look at all well, there's something wrong, I think you ought to go and have a peek at her, I can't say I like the way she was. Why don't you and the others go along there? I left Max to keep his eye on things."

"Don't be so ridiculous, she's resting that's all."

"She had a glass of whisky."

"Oh, Robert, darling, you do make me laugh. Who has ever heard of Auntie May being drunk or who could ever imagine such a thing?"

"I never said she was tight, all I said, or suggested rather, was that you should all go down there where Max is and that your aunt was very ill and needed you probably. I don't care. Where is Angela?"

"Oh, she's got a beau with her, they've wandered off. All right, darling, then I'll go but I don't want the others to know, do you understand, not a word to them. If Auntie May is ill I'll see to it. Now then you stay here."

"What shall I say about you?"

"I'll be back in ten minutes."

Julia came up to Robert with Miss Henderson and said really he had not been very clever, they had found Alex and Angela all for themselves. She then asked him where Claire had gone. He said, oh, she had been called away and that he had found Max, he was in the bar now and, it slipped out so to speak, that was where Claire was going.

"Is that where he is then? Has Claire gone to fetch him?" asked Evelyna.

"No, there was something else, I really don't know where she was going."

Julia said she thought they had better send Edwards for Max. Miss Henderson said Claire would come back and that now they had all found each other it would be madness to separate once more. Julia said again, but wouldn't it be better to send Edwards to fetch Max. At this Edwards broke in and said Mr. Adey had told him to stay where he was and that he would be along himself directly.

Julia said: "Oh, I think it's outrageous," and all were embarrassed and fell silent.

At that three things happened. A large force of police filed in, followed by some of the crowd who had been waiting outside, Alex came back without his driver and the station master marked them as being Miss Wray's party and was bearing down on them. This force of police stamped in and their steps sounded ringing out as though they were on hollow ground. The crowd followed and lined up by where they had halted so you could only see the tops of their helmets. Alex said it was rather hard if they were all of them going to be arrested now, particularly after he had paid for his taxi. Miss Hen-

derson said she thought they ought to give you receipts for payments
of that kind and the station master said:

"Am I by any chance speaking to Miss Julia Wray?"

"Yes."

"Miss Wray, your uncle rang me up to say we were to take particular care of you and your party. Now, I don't like to see you waiting about here in all this crowd, can I not persuade you to wait in the
Hotel? It belongs to the Company and I am sure you will be very
comfortable there."

"That's very nice of you, yes, I think we should love to, but the
only thing is we aren't all together yet you see, that is, the rest of our
party hasn't all arrived."

Alex interrupted, "My dear Angela's just there and we know
where Max is, I think it's a marvellous idea, we could have a fire."

"But what about Max?" Evelyn said.

Alex became agitated at this, he felt he might be prevented from
getting his comforts.

"Bother Max," he said, "what consideration has he shown us?
Why he said he would wait for me at his flat" (this was not true) "to
come on to the station with me, but when I got there I found he was
gone."

Julia asked why they could not get into their train and be off. She
spoke sharply for her. And then they all moved off without discussing that hotel any more, with the station master explaining how this
fog had complicated things. Edwards came to them as they made
their way and Alex brought Angela up with her young man. Edwards asked what he was to do and Julia said: "You can wait for Mr.
Adey, Edwards, as he told you to." Robert said he must go and tell
Claire and he would let Max know as well, and that he would meet
them in the hotel.

After Alex had fetched them and they were making their way back
to the hotel, Robin said to Angela, he supposed they were now going
to dance attendance on Max Adey who, although he was host, had

not had the decency to turn up yet and was probably putting drinks down wherever he was. "Well," Angela said, "and have you ever seen him drunk?" "Of course I have, stinking drunk. My dear girl, what on earth d'you think?" "I bet you haven't, no one ever has. And I suppose you're never tipsy either. I don't know why I have to listen to all this, I wish you'd go and have done with it. You are so tiresome, now go and give me some peace." He went off fast, almost running, not trusting himself to speak. As she came up she told the others self-consciously Robin had had to be off. They paid no attention and she found that Julia had returned to the question of why they could not get into their train and go. After all she said this fog was only twenty feet up, it was not down to ground level and the station master, with that patience he was paid to have, explained again how impossible it was to see one's hand in front of one's face less than three hundred yards south of where they were now. And in this way they got near to the hotel.

Before they went inside Evelyn took charge and sent Robert into the bar to tell Max and Claire where they were going, with instructions that he himself was to come back at once if possible with Max. When they got inside she told the station master she was sure he was very busy and that now they were here they would be quite all right. This was nerves on her part, there was no reason for getting rid of him. Speaking to Julia and not to Evelyna he replied that he must just reserve a room for them, they would be guests of the Company, it was far too crowded for them to stay in any of the public rooms and he made off to that broad open window which had RECEP-TION lit up over it. One pale young man in morning clothes was inside this window and twelve people were bothering him.

"But I thought Max was to be here, where on earth is he?" Julia said. "It's perfectly wicked, here we all are turning up to time and not a sign of him, only that wretched Edwards."

"Here he is now, darling," Angela said and as he came up Mr. Adey said: "There you all are," as if it was they who had been lost and were late.

Evelyna was so relieved she became snappy. She asked him where on earth had he been and he said why here, of course, and Julia, knowing how he disliked other people getting rooms and meals—if he was in a party he would never let anyone else pay for whatever it might be—told him the station master was getting rooms for them.

"Can't have that," he said, and it was one of those things Julia liked about Max, she thought it generous. She went forward with him to the reception desk. The young man in morning clothes recognized Max and, "why Mr. Adey," he said, "are you in the station master's party, what can I do for you?"

"I don't know anything about the station master, I want three sitting rooms."

"All on one floor, Mr. Adey?"

"Of course not. No, two on one floor and one on the floor above."

"I'm afraid they'll have to be with bedrooms, we don't have sitting rooms separate."

"I know, I know. Be quick about it."

In the meantime Julia had tried to explain to her station master that Max would not hear of the Company taking a room for them because he was like that, it was very kind of the station master, it wasn't that she was ungrateful, nor was Max being rude, it was most kind of him to have looked after them and she was sure he must be very busy and ought to get back. When she returned, Max was being given three keys.

"But, darling," she said, "whatever do we want with three rooms?"

"Claire's aunt," he said, "sick."

"Oh no."

"Doesn't want anyone to know."

"How awful."

"Just arranged for three men to carry her up the back way where she won't be seen."

"What on earth is the matter with her, Max, is she bad?"

"Don't know; tight I should say. Look out, here's the others."

As they came up, a hall porter was with them and when he saw it was Max he said to him:

"Same room, sir?"

"No; 95, 96 and 196 this time."

Alex said so this was where he had been hiding, and, tactlessly, what had he wanted with a room before? Max lied again, he said he had had to see his lawyer.

Julia knew he was a liar, it was one of those things one had to put up with when one was with him. But it did seem to her unfair that he should go and spoil it all now that he was here. She had forgotten how much she had resented his not turning up in her pleasure at seeing him, and now he was telling them this fairy tale about his lawyer. People were cruel. But perhaps he had wanted to make his will. Anything might happen to any one of them, everything was so going wrong. As she looked about her, at the other travellers, she could get no comfort out of what she saw. Perhaps he was not lying, which was frightening enough, but if he was then why was he lying? And this time she could not look through her things for charms, they had been left behind with her porter.

She was in a long hall with hidden lighting and, for ornament, a vast chandelier with thousands of glass drops and rather dirty. It was full of people and those who had found seats, which were all of them too low, lay with blank faces as if exhausted and, if there was anything to hope for, as though they had lost hope. Most of them were enormously fat. One man there had a cigar in his mouth, and then she saw he had one glass eye, and in his hand he had a box of matches which now and again he would bring up to his cigar. Just as he was about to strike his match he looked round each time and let his hands drop back to his lap, his match not lighted. Those standing in groups talked low and were rather bent and there was a huge illuminated clock they all kept looking at. Almost every woman was having tea as if she owned the whole tray of it. Almost every man had a dispatch case filled with daily newspapers. She thought it was like an enormous doctor's waiting room and that it would be like that when they were all dead and waiting at the gates.

She saw Claire coming and rushed forward to meet her and cried:

"My darling, my darling, in this awful place I wondered whether we weren't all dead really."

"Julia darling, it is such a bother. I've just come from Auntie May, Robert found her when he was looking for Max and she is not at all well. I don't want a soul to know. I'm very worried about her."

"Claire, I am sorry. Can I do anything?"

"I think we must get her in here, don't you?"

"Of course we must. As a matter of fact I know Max has taken an extra room, well to tell you the truth he's taken three rooms, just like him."

"Yes, he's been very good. He's arranged to have her taken in the back way, poor Auntie May, she can't walk, you see. But nobody must know. Of course, darling, I would be miserable keeping it from you but not a word to another soul, please. Max didn't say anything, did he?"

"No, not to me."

"That's all right then. Darling, I must fly and see that her room is all ready," and when she made off Julia went to where Max was waiting for her to make him swear he would not tell another soul because of Claire.

And now Claire, who had been stopped by Evelyna, was telling her about Miss Fellowes and was swearing her to secrecy. Alex thought something was going on so he came up and he was told on condition that he did not breathe it to anyone. So in the end there was only Miss Crevy and Robin, her young man, who did not know. He would not have cared if they had all become lepers (after going off he had made up his mind he ought to keep his eye on Angela in case she might want him; he was now trying to get in the back way so she could not know he was hanging around). Angela felt very much out of it all. She had noticed, and it was obvious they were keeping secrets from her. Now Robin was gone she felt she had been left on their hands and felt inclined to blame him for going off like that without saying good-bye.

Robert came in and stopped by Julia.

"Do you know about it?" he said.

"Yes, I do."

"Well, they are just carrying her in now."

"Robert, is she very ill, poor thing?"

"I don't know. It's such a bore for Claire."

"Robert, what on earth are they doing to the doors?"

"Oh that? They are putting up steel shutters over the main entrance so they told me when I came in. I say, you know about Claire not wanting anyone to know about her Aunt May? Well, when we were small there was a bamboo patch in the kitchen garden and do you remember we used to imagine there was something out of the way in the middle of it they grew so thick? I was only thinking of it just now. Well, Claire was practically brought up with us, wasn't she, when we were small and when she was sent over to play with us you know we never told her about those bamboos. Curious, wasn't it?"

"But, my dear, they aren't going to shut us up in this awful place, surely? What do they want to put shutters up for and steel ones?"

"It's the fog, I believe. Last time there was bad fog and a lot of people were stuck here they made a rush for this place I believe to get something to eat. Good Lord! it doesn't make you nervous, does it?"

It did make Julia feel very nervous and she moved to Alex where he happened to be teasing Angela because he might be nervous too which would comfort her. People who weren't nervous were useless because they did not know what it meant, but however nervous he was, and if he wasn't then Julia felt she would like to make him be, he would comfort because, after all, he was a man.

There was a crash.

"Good heavens," Alex said, "what's that?"

"It's the steel door," Julia cried, "they've shut it down and how ever Claire will get her—" and then she was silent as she expected Angela did not know. "Oh, Alex dear," she went on, "we're shut in now, what shall we do, isn't it awful?"

He could think of nothing better to say than what do you know about that? There was a hush, everyone in this hall was looking towards that now impenetrable entrance, women held cups half-way to their lips, little fingers of their right hands stuck out pointing towards where that crash had come from. And it was this moment the individual who could not or would not light his cigar chose to light the match in such a way that every match in his box was lit and it exploded. He was so upset his cigar tumbled out of his mouth; it was his moment, everyone now looked at him.

"But how about my claustrophobia?" Alex asked. They all heard the man near them say to his companion, a woman, no, he would certainly do nothing of the kind. And Julia demanded to know about their luggage, was it to be left out there to be looted, for their porters would not protect it.

"It's all too disastrous," Alex said and then when he saw Max, who had come up to them, "my dear," he said to him, "hadn't we all better go home and start another day?"

"Can't get home in this fog. No, I've taken rooms here."

"But, Max, we can't sleep here."

"You won't have to, old boy. Trains will be running soon. Come along, Angela, let's all go up."

"If it wasn't so ludicrous it would be quite comic," Alex said to Julia as they followed. She said she could not go up in the lift, she never could go up in them, would he mind climbing with her? As they went up short flights from landing to landing on deep plush carpets with sofas covered in tartan on each landing, Miss Fellowes was being carried by two hotel porters up the back stairs. For every step Alex and Julia took Miss Fellowes was taken up one too, slumped on one of those chromium-plated seats, her parcel on her lap, followed by the two silent nannies and, coming last, that same man who had sat next her, he who winked.

Max got Angela into one of that pair of rooms he had reserved on one floor so that she could not see Miss Fellowes carried in as Claire seemed so keen on nobody knowing. He said Julia looked a bit down, he had better order drinks.

He telephoned and was just saying:

"Please send up cocktail things. No, I don't want a man, we'll make them ourselves. I want a shaker, some gin, a bottle of Cointreau and some limes. How much? Send up two of everything and about twelve limes. No, no, only one bottle of Cointreau. These people here are fools." He was just saying this as Julia and Alex came in. Julia said:

"She's arrived, Max."

"Who, darling?" Angela asked.

"Oh, no one. Wouldn't you like some tea, darling," she said to Angela, "it might do us all some good. Max, be an angel and tell them to send up some tea." So he ordered tea and said they had better send up whisky and two syphons also. Angela, who did not know them well, wondered at how Julia ordered Max about, and at this room, and at the prodigious number of things he had just sent for and then heard him asking for flowers.

Angela said: "Now Robin isn't here, because you know he is a relation of Embassy Dick's, do tell me, has anyone heard any more about it?"

Alex put her right about that. "Embassy Richard, dear, not Embassy Dick," he said.

"Nonsense, Alex, I think Embassy Dick is a perfectly good name for him and a much better one anyway," said Julia. Max now made one of his observations. "If he was a bird," he said, "he would not last long." Julia asked him what on earth he meant and got no answer. Then Angela went on to say this Richard had met her mother and for no reason at all, that is to say he had no cause to bring it in to what they had been saying, he had told her mother he would not be able to go to that reception. Alex objected that Embassy Richard was always saying things of that kind, it proved nothing, and Julia wondered whether Angela was not inventing it all. "But what I mean is," Angela said, "he made a point of his not being able to go. So don't you see someone who might have heard him and had got to know that he had not been invited saw their chance and sent that notice to the papers."

"But surely, my dear, you don't mean to suggest that he sent the message himself."

"Alex, what do you mean?"

"Look here, Angela, you seem to think that just because someone

overheard him making his alibi about that party it proves that someone else must have sent the notice to the society columns. Well," Alex
went on and so lost track of his argument, "surely that must be so. I
mean no one has ever suggested that he sent the message himself."

"So you said before, so I seem to remember," Julia said, who loved
arguments, "but I don't see any reason for saying he didn't send it
himself."

Alex was very taken with this suggestion and complimented Julia
on it; he said no one had ever thought of it or, at any rate, not in his
hearing. Angela said but surely Embassy Richard wouldn't willingly
have brought all that on himself to which Alex replied by asking
how he could have known the Ambassador would disown him.

"The Ambassador knows him quite well, too."

"All the more reason then, Angela dear," Alex said, "I expect he
was fed up with him."

"Poisonous chap," said Max.

"Max, darling, don't be so aggravating, which one do you mean,
the Ambassador or Richard?"

"Well, after all, Julia, why should he be called Embassy Richard if
he wasn't?" Alex said.

Julia said she did not agree, she thought him very good-looking
and didn't Angela think so too. Angela agreed and Alex said "Oh,
very fetching!"

"No, Alex, don't, you're spoiling the whole argument by attack-
ing him. It's neither here nor there to say that he's awful, what we're
talking about is whether he sent that notice himself."

Max chose this moment to leave the room and again Angela felt
she was out of it, that they were keeping things from her and, as she
thought Alex had been tiresome with her over this argument, she
decided she would rather go for him.

"Anyhow, Alex," she said, "I bet there's one thing you don't know."

"I expect there are several."

"And that is that the Prince Royal is a friend of Richard's and was
frightfully angry with his Ambassador when he saw the letter he
wrote."

"I must say I can't see that makes the slightest difference. Anyway I did know about the Prince what d'you call him. You see, Angela, we were arguing about who could have sent the notice if Embassy Richard didn't sent it for himself. I can't see that it matters two hoots if the Prince Royal was cross."

"I can," said Julia, entering into it again. "I think it's a score for Richard if the Ambassador's employer is cross with him for trying to score off Richard."

"No," and Alex was now speaking in his high voice he used when he was upset, "that's not the point. The real point is that the Ambassador ticked off Embassy Richard in public by writing to the papers to say he had never invited him to his party. If the Prince Royal told his Ambassador off for doing it, it doesn't make any difference to the fact that Richard was shown up in public."

"But Alex, dear, it does," Julia said. "If the Prince Royal did not approve, and the party was being given for him, then it means that Embassy Richard should have been invited all the time."

"I don't see that it does, Julia. He may not have approved of the way his Ambassador did it. My whole point is that the Prince Royal never made his Ambassador write another letter to the papers saying that Richard should have been invited after all. D'you see?"

Angela said "No, Alex, I don't."

"Well, what I mean is that you and I may know the Prince Royal was tremendously angry and threw fits, if you like, when he read his Ambassador's letter but the thousands of people in the street who read their newspapers every morning would not hear about it. All that they know is that Embassy Richard regretted not being able to attend a party he was not invited to."

"Oh, if that's it," said Angela, "then who cares about the people in the street and what they think about it."

They were all silent trying to keep their tempers when Evelyn Henderson came in. They all told her at one time what they had said and what they had meant and when she had gathered what all this was about she said:

"But I don't understand your saying that the Ambassador knew

Richard quite well. You know in that letter of his the newspapers printed he said he had never seen him in his life. And then for the matter of that, isn't the story of Embassy Richard's being a friend of the Prince Royal just the sort of thing Richard would put round to clear himself? Does anyone know, really know, that it's true?"

Angela said well, as a matter of fact, she did know for certain they were friends because her mother knew the Prince Royal well and he had told her so. Alex asked if that was before or after this business about the party and she replied that it was before. He was just about to say the Prince Royal might think very differently about Richard now and Angela was waiting for him—she was in that state she would have accused him of being rude whatever he said—when Alex saw signs of agitation in Evelyn Henderson and guessed she must have news of Miss Fellowes. So, in order to occupy her attention, he began to make peace with Angela while Evelyn drew Julia aside. In a minute these two went out together and Angela, when she saw it, realized how treacherous Alex really was.

When they were outside that room Miss Henderson said to Julia:

"My dear, you look very pale, are you all right?"

"Yes, I think so. I get so excited, up one moment, down the next, you know how it is," and Miss Henderson when she heard this thought poor child, it is in love. She was three years older than Julia. "Well," she said, "what I wanted to tell you and of course I didn't want the others in there to hear, is that poor Claire's aunt is very ill, I'm sure of it."

"Oh dear!"

"Yes. Robert has gone to try and find a doctor. I expect there'll be one stuck in this beastly hotel same as we are. But there's more than that. I'm rather unhappy in my own mind about it. She had a parcel of sorts and as we were getting her on the bed it fell down and came open and there was a pigeon of all things inside."

"A dead pigeon? Perhaps she was taking it back for her supper."

"No, it was all wet."

"Oh, Evelyna, how disgusting! But how could it be wet?"

"That's what I asked myself. But Claire's old nannie, who has been keeping an eye on her tells me she saw Claire's Auntie May washing it in the 'Ladies.'"

"Well, I think that's rather sweet."

"I'm not so sure about that, my darling Julie, and I'd rather you did not say anything to Claire about that part of it. I don't think she knows and she is so upset already, I don't want her worried any more."

"Yes, if you say so, but I don't see anything so very awful in it."

"Good heavens, do you see what I see, those poor old dears are crying. Why," Evelyn said, hurrying up to where those two nannies sat in tears on a settee, "it is being a tiresome difficult day for us all, isn't it?" she said to them. "Now, wouldn't you like a nice cup of tea?"

They made noises which could be taken to mean yes and Julia explained to Miss Henderson how Max had already ordered tea so that it would be easy to carry two cups along to them without Angela knowing. As they moved off down the corridor Evelyn said she did not like the way they were crying, did Julia think Miss Fellowes had done anything? Julia said something or other in reply. She was now struck by how extraordinary it was their being here in this corridor with the South of France, where they were going, waiting for them at the end of their journey. They had all, except for Angela Crevy, been in the same party twelve months ago to the same place, so fantastically different from this. One day would be so fine you wondered if it could be true, the next it rained like anywhere else. But when it was fine you sat on the terrace for dinner looking over a sea of milk with a sky fainting into dusk with the most delicate blushes—Oh! she cried in her heart, if only we could be there now. Indeed, this promise of where they were going lay back of all their minds or feelings, common to all of them. If they did not mention it, it was why they were in this hotel and there was not one of them, except of course for Miss Fellowes and the nannies, who did not every now and again most secretly revert to it.

As for Miss Fellowes, she was fighting. Lying inanimate where they had laid her she waged war with storms of darkness which rolled up over her in a series, like tides summoned by a moon. What made her fight was the one thought that she must not be ill in front of these young people. She did not know how ill she was.

Those nannies, like the chorus in Greek plays, knew Miss Fellowes was very ill. Their profession had been for forty years to ward illness off in others and their small talk had been of sudden strokes, slow cancers, general paralysis, consumption, diabetes and of chills, rheumatism, lumbago, chicken pox, scarlet fever, vaccination and the common cold. They had therefore an unfailing instinct for disaster. By exaggeration, and Fate they found rightly was most often exaggerated, they could foretell from one chilblain on a little toe the gangrene that would mean first that toe coming off, then that leg below the knee, next the upper leg and finally an end so dreadful that it had to be whispered behind hands.

Robert Hignam appeared, asked how his aunt by marriage was and said he thought they would be able to find a doctor for her. Julia said how sorry she felt for Claire, and Robert said yes, it was rather a bore for her. He went on:

"You know, a most extraordinary thing happened about Claire's aunt. You know, Evelyn, you wanted me to go and find Angela and Max. Well, when I found myself outside the bar down there I went in and came up against Max. D'you know the first thing I asked him was whether he had seen Claire's aunt although no one had ever asked me to find her? As a matter of fact Max did not know her by sight but as soon as I'd finished telling him, there she was in a chair, large as life and ill at that."

"I knew all along I'd forgotten something," Julia said, but almost to herself and in so low a voice they did not catch it, "there's Thomson outside now still looking for the others and he's probably looking for us now as well."

Evelyn told Robert it could never be thought-transference as if anyone had been thinking of Miss Fellowes they could not have known she was ill. He said it had made him feel rather uncomfortable and she said she did not see how it made him feel that. "That's all very well," he said, "but wouldn't you if for no reason at all you began asking after someone you had no reason to think of?"

Evelyn was very practical. "But that's just it, Robert," she said, "you had cause to think of her because you had probably seen her unconsciously as you came in, though you did not realize it at the time, and that is what made you ask after her."

And now Julia, who had been worrying about Thomson, got to that pitch like when a vessel is being filled it gets so full the water spills over. Julia broke in, saying but what about Thomson, he was sent out with you Robert, what's happened to him?

"Half a tick, Julia. No, look here, Evelyn, if I had seen her subconsciously as you say I would not have been so surprised when I did realize she was there."

"But how do you know?"

"Oh, bother you two and your questions," said Julia. "What am I to do about Thomson? Now that they have put that steel door down over the hotel he won't be able to find us or anyone."

Miss Henderson suggested he might have gone back to their luggage.

"Robert, I wonder if you will do something for me," Julia said. "Could you go to the station master, no, of course you can't get outside. But you could telephone to him, couldn't you and say it's for me, and ask him to send someone out to look for Thomson and tell him that he must go back at once to where the luggage is and tell him to see my porter does not put it in the cloakroom if we are a long time. I told my porter that he must not put it in the cloakroom whatever happened, I don't trust these places, but you know what these porters are. Robert, will you do that for me?"

"Yes, only too glad to. But I say, Julia, you know that station master must be a pretty busy man, what with the fog and everything. What do you think?"

"He'll be glad to do it because of my uncle. It would be ever so sweet of you, my dear."

Miss Fellowes, in her room, felt she was on a shore wedged between two rocks, soft and hard. Out beyond a grey sea with, above, a darker sky, she would notice small clouds where sea joined sky and these clouds coming far away together into a darker mass would rush across from that horizon towards where she was held down. As this cumulus advanced the sea below would rise, most menacing and capped with foam, and as it came nearer she could hear the shrieking wind in throbbing through her ears. She would try not to turn her eyes down to where rising waves broke over rocks as the nearer that black mass advanced so fast the sea rose and ate up what little was left between her and those wild waters. Each time this scene was repeated she felt so frightened, and then it was menacing and she throbbed unbearably, it was all forced into her head; it was so menacing she thought each time the pressure was such her eyes would be forced out of her head to let her blood out. And then when she thought she must be overwhelmed, or break, this storm would go back and those waters and her blood recede, that moon would go out above her head, and a sweet tide washed down from scalp to toes and she could rest.

"My dear Mr. Hinham," the station master said to Robert, for he had not caught his name, "My dear sir, there are now, we estimate, thirty thousand people in the station. The last time we had a count, on the August Bank Holiday of last year, we found that when they really began coming in, nine hundred and sixty-five persons could enter this station by the various subways each minute. So supposing I sent a man out to look for the individual Thomson, and he did not find him in ten minutes, there would be forty thousand people to choose from. A needle in a—a needle in a—" and he was searching for some better word, "a haystack," he said at last, at a loss.

"I know," said Robert.

"So you see, sir, I'm afraid we can't," the station master said, and quickly rang off before his temper got the better of him.

Miss Crevy asked Alex where everyone had got to, and he said he could not think where they could be. She asked him outright if anything had happened to anybody, and then, because this question seemed awkward, especially as whatever it was that had happened was obviously being kept from her, she lost her grip and fell further into it by asking him did he know what had become of her Robin. She knew she had been thinking of him without realizing it, all this time.

"But he's gone, Angela."

"Oh, yes, of course, he had to go away."

To tide over her embarrassment Alex suggested they might mix the cocktails now.

"But Max isn't here," she said.

"That doesn't matter. He won't mind."

Because of all that had gone before, she said:

"But it's rude to drink other people's cocktails before they come in. You wouldn't go into someone else's house..." and she stopped there, realizing, of course, he probably would if he knew them well enough. She felt miserable. Alex had been so tiresome about Embassy Richard—she must remember to call him by his proper name—and they were all conspiring together to keep something or other from her and then she had shown about Rob, everyone now would think they were engaged. And it was really so rude to start on his drinks without Max being there.

As for Alex he was frantic that she had been asked on their party. People one hardly knew were always putting one in false positions. It would have been too offensive, though so tempting, to reply that naturally one could go into someone's house and drink their drink, not champagne, of course, but why not gin and lime juice, everyone else did. And besides, it was a question of how well you knew the person, it was intolerable that he should be put wrong because she did not know Max well. It was true that people used not to do it, but when one was in the schoolroom one did not suck one's fingers after jam; on account of one's sisters' governess one wiped them, but one sucked them now, one was grown up.

"I'm sorry, I'm afraid I'm being tiresome," she said. "But this journey is being so long, isn't it? I think I'm going out for a minute."

"Oh, don't go," was all he could think of saying, and she all but said try and stop me if you can, I could knock you down, but she did no more than look away as she went by him.

When she went out into that corridor she had made up her mind she must go home. She felt she had only been invited so they could humiliate her; not that Max would ever do such things, it was the others. Then she saw the nannies, who were still crying. Poor ducks, she thought, have they been vile to them too, how really beastly, poor old things and one of them Claire's nanny. She went up and said,

"There, there, it will be quite all right."

But they would not cry in front of a stranger, and she was surprised and rather hurt to find their tears were drying up, and in two moments she saw they would be putting their handkerchiefs away. Even their nannies, she thought, even their nannies are in league to make one feel out of it. At that instant the man who had been with Miss Fellowes in the bar, and had spoken to her and watched her, and who had followed when she had been carried up, reappeared walking slowly up the corridor. His head was bent forward. He stared at those nannies when he was close to them. He stopped and then, for the first time, he looked at her.

"Ah, they carried 'er up here. Terrible bad she was then, I reckon."

There was a long silence. He went on:

"On one of them stools with backs to 'em there was in the bar."

Alex had come out after Angela. It upset him to see this man. He spoke in his high voice he had when he was upset.

"What are you doing here?" he said.

"What's that to you, my lad?"

"Why don't you go away? These are private rooms here."

"Aye, but the corridor's public," this man returned, and without any warning he had used Yorkshire accent where previously he had been speaking in Brummagem. This sudden change did his trick as it had so often done before and Alex, losing his nerve, asked him in to have a drink. He thought he might be the hotel detective.

"What'll you have?"

"I don't mind," this man said, speaking this time in an educated voice.

"I'm afraid everything must seem very odd to you," said Alex, "I mean there seems to be so much going on, but you see we are all going on a party together abroad, and now here we are stuck in this hotel on account of fog."

It was difficult for Alex. He had come out after Angela because he could never stand things being left in what he called false positions. He was friendly by nature and if he could not help feeling annoyed with Miss Crevy and having digs at her, particularly when she tried to put him in the wrong as he now felt she was continually trying to do, he did not want her to bear him a grudge. It was as much this particularity of his which led him to entertain the mystery man as it was his feeling that he might make trouble for Miss Fellowes if he was not kept amused. While he busily talked with this little man he kept on despairing of ever getting things straight with Angela.

Miss Crevy stood outside with those two nannies, who were also standing up now. She was not so anxious to get home. She was wondering what could be going on that they would not tell her. Then Claire came out with a man who was too obviously the hotel doctor. He looked at Angela with suspicion, and walking down that corridor he said to Claire, quietly:

"What relation is the lady I have just examined to you?"

"She is my aunt."

"I see, I see."

"What are we to do?" Claire asked him. "It really is such a bore poor Auntie May getting like this, and it seems quite impossible to get her out of here. It was extraordinarily lucky that we were able to get hold of you. But, of course, it is too tiresome for her, I can't think of anything worse, can you, than being ill in a hotel bedroom? It was so lucky I did go where they told me I'd find her, because I could see at once she was very ill. What do you think of her?"

"Has she been drinking any stimulants, within the last hour shall we say?"

"Why, yes, I think someone said she had."

"Well, I don't think you need worry about her. It would be a good thing if she could get some sleep. Keep her warm, of course. Oh, yes, it will pass off. Perhaps I might see your husband, wasn't it, for a moment?"

When Robert Hignam came out this doctor drew him aside and said that would be ten and sixpence, please. Claire sent those nannies in to watch Miss Fellowes telling them there was nothing to worry over in her condition, which they did not believe, and she told Julia who was there, too, that it was nothing, and they could go back to that other room and have a drink. Max had come back after trying unsuccessfully to get an ambulance to take Miss Fellowes home (it appeared the streets were so choked with traffic that no communication was possible) and Robert having paid the doctor they all, with Angela, came into the room where Alex was pouring drinks.

As they came in, Robert was explaining to Julia how impossible it was for any search to be made for Thomson. She said:

"Good heavens, who's that?"

They saw facing them that little man, with his glass of whisky, and in the other hand a shabby bowler hat. His tie was thin, as thin as him, and his collar clean and stiff, and so was he; his clothes were black, and his face white with pale, blue eyes. Compared to them he looked like another escaped poisoner, and as if he was looking out for victims. Alex, in the silence this man had made with his appearance, asked him loudly if he would have another drink, and this time he nodded, as though he did not want to speak until he could make up his mind which accent would do his trick best this time.

After she had glanced at Max and seen that he did not seem to care either way about the little man being there, Julia decided it was best to ignore him.

"But are you sure you gave my name?" she said to Robert.

"Yes, I did, and he said he felt you would understand."

"But what about poor Thomson's tea? He is most frightfully particular about that."

"Well, after all, he can get some for himself," and Robert thought it was absurd. Julia would say nothing of keeping Thomson up for something or other until three in the morning, why start this game about tea?

Angela said to Max:

"Darling, who is that man?"

"Don't know."

"But then why is Alex giving him drinks?"

"Don't care, do you?"

"Max, darling, is there any chance of going home do you think? I mean, it does seem to be rather hopeless hanging about here."

"No chance at all. I couldn't even get an ambulance for Claire's aunt."

"What, is she ill?"

"Didn't you know?"

"Yes, darling, didn't you know?" Claire said. "But the doctor says there is nothing the matter with her really. Rest would put her right, he said."

Alex was overjoyed, and said why, that was splendid, loudly, and that little man did not seem pleased, gulped down his drink and left them, saying, in Brummagem, she had been cruel bad when he seen her last.

"Who on earth was that, Alex?"

"My dear Julia, I'm perfectly sure it was the hotel detective."

"But why?"

"Why? But don't you see that if this Miss Fellowes had been really bad, and he had found out he would have insisted on having her moved."

"I don't see at all."

"They won't have people, well, people who are very bad in hotels."

Claire asked who had said her Aunt May was very bad, and Alex could only say his little man had. Angela said "Oh, well, if you will believe what he said," and Julia took that up and said she thought Alex had been perfectly right. Angela, trying to be malicious and yet not rude, said she was horrified to hear Miss Fellowes had been ill, and that she had only remarked to Robin Adams when they met her how she had not seemed right. Alex wanted to ask Miss Crevy where Mr. Adams was, but he did not dare, and Claire said yes, she knew, but she thought it so awful of people to saddle others with their family troubles, Max had been perfectly sweet to put her aunt in a room of her own, but it did seem so unfair that all the rest of them should be bothered by it. "So I didn't tell you," she said to Angela, and in so doing, gave herself away, for she had at first seemed surprised that Miss Crevy did not know. And Miss Crevy, thinking to withdraw and be nice, said well, poor Miss Fellowes could not help herself feeling ill could she, and, sensing that she must have said the wrong thing, she added that whenever she felt ill she consoled herself with those sentiments.

"But, darling, why did you think he was a hotel detective?" Julia said to Alex.

"Because he had a bowler hat, of course," said Claire. "If Alex will go to so many films where they are the only people who do wear bowlers, of course, that's how he gets it into his head. No, you needn't be embarrassed, I know exactly how it was, you couldn't have told how ill she was, and I think it was perfectly sweet of you to have looked after this man like you did, and like that angel Evelyna is looking after Auntie May this moment. And that reminds me that I must go back and relieve poor Evelyn, I shan't be long," and with that she left. Alex felt better but not entirely justified so he asked Julia why she was so certain it could not have been a detective. Julia, however, had seen Max put his arm round Angela Crevy and draw her to the window where they now stood looking down at crowds beneath. Alex did not find that Julia was giving him her attention.

Angela said to Max, speaking confidentially, that she was having a marvellous time, even if it was a bit overwhelming occasionally. He said he was glad. She went on that it would be so marvellous to be really off, that is, in their train and on their way, with the sun waiting for them where they were going, and that she adored going in boats, other people hated Channel crossings, but for her they were more fun than all the rest of her journey. He squeezed her in reply.

"Max, darling, where's our tea?" Julia asked.

He apologized and, going to the telephone, he got on to the management. When he had finished, and they had finally apologized this voice said:

"Oh, Mr. Adey, a lady has been ringing up to ask if you put a call through to her."

"Well?"

"We said that you had not done so"

Max said right and putting his arm round Julia this time he led her to the window. Looking down she saw the whole of that station below them, lit now by electricity, and covered from end to end by one mass of people. "Oh, my dear!" she said, "poor Thomson." As those people smoked below, or it might have been the damp off their clothes evaporating rather than their cigarettes, it did seem like November sun striking through mist rising off water. Or, so she thought, like those illustrations you saw in weekly papers, of corpuscles in blood, for here and there a narrow stream of people shoved and moved in lines three deep and where they did this they were like veins. She wondered if this were what you saw when you stood on your wedding day, a Queen, on your balcony looking at subjects massed below.

"It's like being a Queen," she told Max. He squeezed her.

"You didn't do anything about Edwards, did you?" she said and he did not reply.

She saw the electric trains drawn up in lines with no one on their platforms, everyone was locked out behind barriers and she thought, too, how wonderful it would be when they had arrived.

Alex came up and said what they saw now was like a view from the gibbet and she exclaimed against that. And Miss Fellowes wearily faced another tide of illness. Aching all over she watched helpless while that cloud rushed across to where she was wedged and again the sea below rose with it, most menacing and capped with foam and as it came nearer she heard again the shrieking wind in throbbing through her ears. In terror she watched the seas rise to get at her, so menacing her blood throbbed unbearably, and again it was all forced into her head but this had happened so often she felt she had experienced the worst of it. But now with a roll of drums and then a most frightful crash lightning came out of that cloud and played upon the sea, and this was repeated, and then again, each time nearer till she knew she was worse than she had ever been. One last crash which she knew to be unbearable and she burst and exploded into complete insensibility. She vomited.

"Come away for a minute," Max said to Julia. As they went off and passed that door it opened and Claire came out with Evelyna. Both of them were smiling and said she would do better now, now she had done what the doctor said.

As she walked down that corridor with Max, and he still had his arm round her, she wondered so faintly she hardly knew she had it in her mind where he could be taking her and all the while she was telling him about her charms, her mood softening and made expansive by his having taken her away.

Max was dark and excessively handsome, one of those rich young men who when still younger had been taken up by an older woman, richer than himself. Money always goes to money, the poor always marry someone poorer than themselves, but it is only the rich who rule worlds such as we describe and no small part of Max's attraction lay in his having started so well with someone even richer than himself.

It was generally believed that he had lived with this rich lady, there was hardly anyone who would not have sworn this was the case, and indeed they were on such terms that both were glad to admit they had. As it happened they had on no occasion had anything to do with each other.

It follows that, having begun so well, Max had by now become extraordinarily smart in every sense and his reputation was that he went to bed with every girl. Through being so rich he certainly had more chances. He took them and, of serious offers accepted, his most recent had been Amabel.

Max therefore was reckoned to be of importance, he was well known, he moved in circles made up of people older than himself, and there was no girl of his own age like Julia, Claire Hignam or Miss Crevy—even Evelyna Henderson although she was hardly in it—who did not feel something when they were on his arm, particularly when he was so good-looking. Again one of his attractions was that they all thought they could stop him drinking, not that he ever got drunk because he had not yet lost his head for drink, but they were all sure that if they married him they could make him into something quite wonderful, and that they could get him away from all those other women, or so many of them as were not rather friends of their own. It was for this therefore she made out it meant something to be going on this trip, that it was fun to be walking down this corridor, getting him away from the others, or that was all she would admit she found about him who was more than anyone to her.

"So I went back, darling, and I asked my darling Jemima where could she have put my charms," Julia said, leaning on him a little, "and she promised me faithfully they were in my cabin trunk. Are you like that, have you anything you don't like to travel without? Not toothbrushes or sponges I mean, but things you can't use, like mascots." At this they came to some stairs and the lift.

"Where on earth are you taking me?" she said.

"Got some tea for you in a special room."

People were going up and down so he took his arm off her as they came up and rang for the lift. She had forgotten, through being with him, her dislike of going in these. As they got out on the next floor she was thinking no one else would have bothered to spare her walking up one flight of stairs.

"Yes, so then I had to simply fly back, in a taxi this time, as I was terrified I was going to miss you all. You know I've never never done anything so eerie as walking through the Park in the dark when it was only four o'clock or whatever time it was. The extraordinary part was the birds who had gone to sleep as they thought it was night and then were woken up by the car lights so they muttered in their sleep, the darlings, just like Jemima tells me I do when she pulls the blinds. I got so frightened. And then do you know I imagined what I should say to you if I met you walking alone there. But that was silly and then I remembered about my charms and went back to the house like I told you."

They came to the room he had reserved.

"Oh, tea, tea!" she cried as she went in and clapped her hands, "tea and crumpets, how divine of you, darling, and so grand, just for us two. You know I think I will take my hat off," and doing this she wandered round looking at pictures on the walls.

One of these was of Nero fiddling while Rome burned, on a marble terrace. He stood to his violin and eight fat women reclined on mattresses in front while behind was what was evidently a great conflagration.

"Nero and his wives," she said and passed on.

Another was one of those reproductions of French eighteenth-century paintings which showed a large bed with covers turned back and half in, half out of it a fat girl with fat legs sticking out of her nightdress and one man menacing and another disappearing behind curtains.

"Here's a to-do," she said.

Another was of a church, obviously in Scotland, and snow and sheep, at the back of a bleak mountain, fir trees in the middle distance and you could see church bells were ringing, they were at an angle in the belfry.

"Oh, do look, Max darling, come here. Isn't that like the church at Barshottie which you took last winter, do you remember?" And then as he put his arm round her again she said: "No, don't do that, it's too hot in here. Let's have some tea or my crumpets will be cold."

When she was pouring him out his tea she asked him if he had heard anything about Embassy Richard. Speaking slowly in his rather low voice he said he understood that there had been a girl this man had wanted to see at that party. She wanted to know who that might be but he would not tell her although she pressed him; she approved of his not giving this girl's name away, it proved to her that he was safe.

"But Max, my dear," she said, "surely the point is that Embassy Richard didn't go to the party. Some people think he sent that notice to the papers himself saying he could not attend, and if he did that then he can't have meant to go."

"All I know is he's head over heels in love with this girl," Mr. Adey said, "and he was not invited and she was, and he meant to go whether he got his invitation or not."

"But my dear how absolutely thrilling; then why didn't he go?"

"What I heard was that Charlie Troupe, who knew of this, rang him up to say his girl was not going after all but would be at the Beavis's dance."

"I see. All the same, Max, he had only to ring up his friend to see if she was going or not."

"No, he had had a row with her."

"Then if what you say is right it does look like Charlie Troupe after all, I mean it does seem as though it was Charlie Troupe who sent that notice out. But if you won't tell me the name of the girl I shall still go on believing that Richard did it himself."

"Believe it or not, it's true that he didn't and I call it a dirty trick to play."

"When he was in love, you mean," she said. "But that's just the time people do play dirty tricks," and at this she looked very knowledgeable.

"On each other, yes, but it's not playing the game for a third person to do it."

"Perhaps Charlie Troupe was in love with her himself. If you would only tell me her name I'd know."

"I don't hold any brief for Charlie Troupe or Embassy Richard but I think it was a low-down trick," he said.

"People do play awful tricks on each other when they are in love, don't they, Max? I can't understand why people can't go on just being ordinary to each other even if they are in love." She became quite serious. "After all, it's the most marvellous thing that can happen to a person, to two people, there's no point in making it all beastly. You know that thing of making up to someone else so as to make the one you really mind about more mad about you, well, I think that's simply too awful, and very dangerous after all."

He laughed and asked her if she did that after all, and she laughed and said now he was asking questions. She went on, "perhaps that girl friend of Embassy Richard's was trying to hot him up with Charlie Troupe, that would fit in with your idea that it was Charlie Troupe who sent the notice out, but if she was, then I think she deserves everything she gets. Why don't you like Embassy Richard?"

"I don't know, but look at his name. Always crawling round Embassies. And you can see him any night there isn't one of those grander shows on, crawling round night clubs with older women old enough to be his grandmother."

At this she thought how odd it was that people always seemed to dislike in others just what they were always doing themselves, for Max went everywhere at night with older women. Then, to get this conversation back to herself, however indirectly, she said:

"But perhaps Charlie Troupe is only going about like that to make some girl jealous."

"Not Charlie Troupe."

"I don't know," she said, "don't you be too sure. What do we know about anyone?" said she, thinking of herself.

"Not Charlie Troupe."

"Oh, all right. In fact I'm very glad. I think it's perfectly horrible and very wrong to walk out with a third person just because you are in love with another. It's not playing fair. After all, it's the most marvellous thing that can happen to anyone, or at any rate that's what they say," she said to cover her tracks, "and to make a point of making the real person jealous is simply beastly," she said with great sincerity.

Meanwhile Mr. Robin Adams, Miss Angela Crevy's young man, sat in a bar downstairs in this hotel and wondered angrily how Angela could go with these revolting people. Here they were engaged, even if it was not yet in the papers he had her word for it, she would not take his ring but she had said she would be engaged to him when she came back from this trip of theirs, so they must be engaged. And then in spite of it she would insist on going off although she knew he did not approve, although she knew it gave him pain, agony in fact; it was perfectly damnable and made him miserable, it was so unfair. At this moment Robert Hignam hit him hard between the shoulders.

"Robin, old boy, I didn't know you were here," he said. "Have you got sick of them upstairs too? Well, I don't mind telling you I've been sent on so many damn messages, fatigues and things, I said to myself it's time you took a rest and went downstairs and got yourself a drink. Not that old Max hasn't seen to the liquid refreshment, there's plenty of that up there—a small Worthington, please miss—but I should be sent off on some message or other for certain the moment I settled down. It's Claire's aunt, you know. Came to see us off and the doctor here says she's tight or so he gave me to believe, and charged me ten-and-six. That's all tommy rot, you understand, there's something more wrong with her than just that, but I'm not telling the girls; one doesn't want them to get upset. But I must tell you," he went on, thinking poor old Robin seemed a bit glum about something, "the most extraordinary thing happened about Claire's aunt. I'd been sent off to see whether I couldn't find Angela and you and someone else, I forget which of them it was, and I was finding it pretty dry work so I dropped into the bar outside there. Mind you, no one had said a word to me about Claire's aunt but d'you know the first thing I asked Max—I found him sitting there having one before me—was whether he had seen the old lady. And the next thing was I saw her sitting right in the corner and looking pretty queer, too, I can tell you. Bit of an extraordinary thing, wasn't it?"

"Funny thing," Mr. Adams said and he had not listened.

"Yes, that's what the doctor said," Miss Evelyn Henderson was telling Alex, "and now, between ourselves, she has been vomiting so if what the doctor says is right she ought to be getting better."

"Well, that's splendid."

"Yes, but I'm not so sure that doctor knew what he was talking about. Don't go and tell anyone, but she was such a bad colour."

"Evelyn, my dear," Alex said, "don't put your opinion against the doctor's, it's perfectly fatal. If he said what was wrong with her as he did then that's what is the matter, never mind what you or I think. I'm not sure that I agree with you, in any case it's quite likely she had one too many, probably she felt tired and let it get the better of her."

He mixed himself another drink.

"Now don't you go and get drunk too," she said. "I can't have two drunks on my hands."

He laughed and then, because she had rather annoyed him, he made this suggestion:

"Why don't you let Claire look after her? After all she is her niece."

"My dear, Claire couldn't look after a sick cat. As it is I don't know what I should have done if it hadn't been for her old nanny and the friend. They have been simply wonderful. Of course it was they who put me on the track of it and I didn't have a chance of taking that doctor aside, but I don't think they are satisfied either."

"What do you mean?"

"No, I should not have said that. I think you are quite right that I should take what the doctor said," she said to close the subject.

"Well," said Alex, "I have been doing my bit too. A most extraordinary individual blew in here a short time back and I took him for the hotel detective. I thought he was trying to nose out something about this Miss Fellowes. So I buckled to and began plying him with drinks and the others have been chaffing me about it."

"I think you were quite right, perfectly right. It would be dreadful if there was a scandal. Now I must go back. I don't mean a scandal, that's not the right word, a fuss. Now I must go back in there. You go and talk to Angela, she's sitting all alone," and with that Miss Henderson went off.

Upstairs Max and Julia had finished their tea and, in an interval of silence, she had gone over to the window and was looking down on that crowd below. As he came over to join her she said well anyway, those police over there would protect their luggage, as they were drawn up in front of the Registration Hall. And as she watched she saw this crowd was in some way different. It could not be larger as there was no room, but in one section under her window it seemed to be swaying like branches rock in a light wind and, paying greater attention, she seemed to hear a continuous murmur coming from it. When she noticed heads everywhere turned towards that section just below she flung her window up. Max said: "Don't go and let all that in," and she heard them chanting beneath: "WE WANT TRAINS, WE WANT TRAINS." Also that raw air came in, harsh with fog and from somewhere a smell of cooking, there was a shriek from somewhere in the crowd, it was all on a vast scale and not far above her was that vault of glass which was blue now instead of green, now that she was closer to it. She had forgotten what it was to be outside, what it smelled and felt like, and she had not realized what this crowd was, just seeing it through glass. It went on chanting WE WANT TRAINS, WE WANT TRAINS from that one section which surged to and fro and again that same woman shrieked, two or three men were shouting against the chant but she could not distinguish words. She thought how strange it was when hundreds of people turned their heads all in one direction, their faces so much lighter than their dark hats, lozenges, lozenges, lozenges.

The management had shut the steel doors down because when once before another fog had come as thick as this hundreds and hundreds of the crowd, unable to get home by train or bus, had pushed into this hotel and quietly clamoured for rooms, beds, meals, and more and more had pressed quietly, peaceably in until, although they had been most well behaved, by weight of numbers they had smashed everything, furniture, lounges, reception offices, the two bars, doors. Fifty-two had been injured and compensated and one of them was a little Tommy Tucker, now in a school for cripples, only fourteen years of age, and to be supported all his life at the railway company's expense by order of a High Court Judge.

"It's terrifying," Julia said, "I didn't know there were so many people in the world."

"Do shut the window, Julia."

"But why? Max, there's a poor woman down there where that end of the crowd's swaying. Did you hear her call? Couldn't you do something about it?"

He leaned out of the window.

"Couldn't get down there I'm afraid, doors are shut," he said.

At that she closed this window and said he was quite right and that it was silly of her to suggest it. "After all," she said, "one must not hear too many cries for help in this world. If my uncle answered every begging letter he received he would have nothing left in no time." It was extraordinary how quiet their room became once that window was shut. "What do you do with your appeals and things?" He answered that everything was in the hands of his secretary. He decided with his accountants, who managed his affairs for him, what he would set aside for charities during the year and then he told his secretary which ones he wanted to support and his accountants had to approve the actual amount before it was paid. He explained this rather disjointedly and gave her to understand that it was his secretary who really decided everything for him.

"And your accountants, or whatever you call them, decide how much it is to be?"

"That's right."

"Then do you actually spend less than you receive?"

"I don't know."

"But you must know."

"No, I don't. You see my accountants report to my trustees."

"Then don't your trustees tell you?"

"They made a bit of a stink years ago when they said I'd spent too much. It was then they fixed up this system. They haven't said anything since so I suppose it's all right. Will you have a cocktail or something?"

She refused. She began to feel rather uncomfortable in this closed room. He asked if she would mind his sending for some whisky and telephoned down for it.

"Ask them if there is any chance of there being some trains running soon." He reported that they said not for another hour or two, although this fog seemed to be lifting along the coast. She wondered what she had better do, whether her best plan was not to ring up her uncle to say they were all stuck in this hotel, whether it would not be safer supposing he found out they had spent hours penned up alone in here. But then, she argued, it was not as if they were not in a party and no one knew she was up here with Max. And if her uncle told her to come back home then she might not catch their train if it did in the end go off rather unexpectedly. How frightfully rich Max must be. No, it would be better if she stayed where she was, she was not going to miss this trip for anything. She had been looking forward to it for weeks. And besides she wondered, she wondered what he was going to do now that he had her all alone. It made the whole trip so much more exciting to begin with a whole three weeks before them to get everything right in.

"Cheer up," Alex said to Miss Crevy, going up to where she sat alone in that room downstairs, "don't look so glum, Angela."

"Do I?" she said, and she put up her hands to rearrange her hair. "Yes, I suppose I do feel low." In actual fact she felt so low she could not be angry with him any more, though she did still resent him.

"Are you sure," he said, "that you won't have anything to drink?" When she refused he went on that this kind of breakdown in the arrangements was typical of all travelling with Max. "Have you ever been on a trip with him before?" She said she had, which he was pretty certain was a lie. He went on:

"I remember last year, when we were going to the same place we are going now, there was the most frightful business in Paris because all our sleepers weren't together. He had reserved the whole of one coach and when we all got to the train he found they had put us all over it. He made a great row and for some time he threatened not to take the train. Of course, they said he could do exactly as he liked but that he would have to pay for those sleepers in any case and there weren't any others for four days the trains were so full. Well, you know it didn't matter in the least to us where we were, they were single sleepers anyway, but he wouldn't have it and we all stood there thinking perhaps we would never go after all."

"It was rather sweet of him."

"Yes," said Alex, "it was." Alex was anxious to be on good terms with everyone and did not want to remember that Miss Crevy had got on his nerves. "Yes, in many ways he is too good a host, that was why he was so anxious no one should know about Claire's aunt," he said, embroidering, "so that no one should be bothered about anyone else being ill. D'you know," he said, "I've been thinking it over and I think you were quite right about Embassy Richard, that he didn't send that notice out himself."

"All I said was," Angela said rather wearily, "he had told my mother that he was not going to the party."

"That's just it, so I don't think that he could have sent the notice out himself in view of what you have just told me. I quite forget what I said at the time but it's obvious you were right about that and that I was wrong," he said, ignoring altogether that he had originally agreed with her on this point although he had then rather lost track of his argument. But he was anxious to be friends.

"Oh, don't let's talk about that, Alex. But then what happened about the sleepers, did you go in the end?"

"Good heavens, yes, of course we went. They compromised by putting some of us together. Oh, yes, one always goes but it's a certainty something perfectly appalling crops up like this fog or the business about sleepers or any one of the hundreds of things that turn up when he travels. I'm not saying that one isn't exceedingly comfortable, but it's definitely wearing."

He thought to himself that she was not posing to be such an expert on travelling with Max after all. Perhaps she had been once to Scotland with him.

"Have you ever been to Barshottie?"

"No," she said, "why do you ask?"

Miss Fellowes was better. She was having a perfectly serene dream that she was riding home, on an evening after hunting, on an antelope between rows of giant cabbages. Earth and sky were inverted, her ceiling was an indeterminate ridge and furrow barely lit by crescent moons in the azure sky she rode on.

In the sitting-room next to where she lay dreaming watched by those two nannies, Claire and Evelyn discussed Angela's looks, which they admired, and her clothes, of which they did not think so much.

"But, darling," said Claire, "why do you think Max asked her?"

"Why, for that matter, did he ask us?"

"Oh, but Evelyna, we've all known him for ages."

"Yes, but surely to goodness he can get to know someone else. I think we're all unfair to him."

"How do you mean?"

"Well, my dear, of course we're all hoping he'll get engaged to Julia and I don't know if it's because of that but I do think we seem to be getting almost proprietary about him. After all, Claire, he's independent enough now with all these creatures he goes about with at night. He's been most good to me taking me about when I couldn't possibly have afforded to go alone and I can't question who he asks besides."

"I can't either," Claire said, "but I can't help wondering. And anyway," she said, rising in her own defence, "I don't think because Robert and I and you are asked that's any reason why we shouldn't discuss him."

"I know just what you mean but we seem to be doing it all the time nowadays. Not with Julia though, she never talks about him now. Has she said anything to you about him lately?"

"No, Julia is most frightfully close about herself," Claire said. "She's never so much as breathed a word to me ever, has she to you?"

"No, not a word."

"Then you mean what I mean, that she doesn't discuss him now because she minds?"

"Well, of course she does. We knew she did months ago."

"I know, but it is too divine, isn't it?" Claire said and then described how Julia had suddenly said to her about how hopeless Max was, when they were sitting outside together on their luggage.

"Still," said Evelyn, "that's just what people do do."

"What?"

"Talk about their affairs when they are really upset about them."

"Well, Evelyn my dear, she did sort of let it out to me when we were sitting there as I've just told you."

"I didn't mean that. What I meant was really having it out. And that she has never done with any of us."

"Julia's not the same as everyone, that's why she is so sweet."

"Well, Claire, I think we are all the same about things like that, and she's never really had it out with any of us."

If Julia had wondered where Max was taking her as they went up-stairs together Max, for his part, had wondered where she was taking him. With this difference however, that, if she had done no more than ask herself what room he was taking her to, he had asked him-self whether he was going to fall for her. Again, while she had won-dered so faintly she hardly knew she had it in her mind or, in other words, had hardly expressed to herself what she was thinking, he was much further from putting his feelings into words, as it was not until he felt sure of anything that he knew what he was thinking of. When he thought, he was only conscious of uneasy feelings and he only knew that he had been what he did not even call thinking when his feelings hurt him. When he was sure then he felt it must at once be put to music, which was his way of saying words.

This is not to say that Max was one of those men with ungovern-able actions in that sense in which one speaks of men with ungov-ernable tempers, always breaking out into rages. He was not so often sure he was in love with anyone that he was always assaulting girls. But when he was sure then he felt he had to do something.

Julia, of course, he had been continually meeting for eighteen months. He had brought her along when they had been abroad be-fore, though he had not seen much of her then, but since that time he had met her again and again at houses where he happened to be staying and when they had been a great deal more together than with the other guests.

"Tell me about your toys," he said.

"My toys, what do you mean? Oh, you're trying to say my charms. No, I certainly won't if you call them my toys."

"Your charms," he said.

"Well, if you swear you won't laugh I might." She was most anx-ious to tell him because she naturally wanted to talk about herself.

"I won't laugh," he said.

"I don't know how I first got them," she said, for she was not going to tell anyone ever that it was her mother, of course, who had given them to her and who had died when she was two years old. Here she broke off to ask him if he had overheard Robert Hignam telling her about that patch of bamboos they had played round as children. "He is so silly, as if I should ever forget," she said. "We were brought up together." She went on to say what Robert had never known was that one of her charms, the wooden pistol, had been buried plumb in the middle of the bamboo patch. In consequence, and no one had ever known of it, these bamboos, or probably they had been overgrown artichokes, had taken on a great importance in her mind because of this secret buried in them. And she asked Max if he did not think it often was the case that certain things people remembered about when they were children were important to them only because they were far more important to someone else.

She explained that each time they went through those artichokes pretending they were explorers in jungles, she was excited because she knew she had buried her pistol there and because the others did not know. She felt her excitement had made their game more secret and that it was the secrecy which was what Robert remembered of it. "So that it was my having hidden the pistol there which made the whole thing for him. He'll never know," she said.

So her wooden pistol was stained and had rather crumbled away, after she had dug it up, but she had it still, nothing would ever part her from it. The egg she described as being hollow, painted outside with rings of red and yellow, half the size of duck's eggs, and it had inside three little ivory elephants. "You'll never believe about my egg," she said, "and I've never told another soul," which was a lie. But she did tell him, and it was like this. When she had been no more than four years old she had been out with her nanny for their afternoon's walk. She was carrying a huge golfing umbrella she could not be happy without at that particular time, quartered in red and yellow silk. Her nanny had opened it for her and she was so very small she had had to carry it with both hands to the handle as it spread above her head. Now she also had with her the wooden egg with elephants inside in one of her pockets and as she happened to be walking on a bank a sudden gust of wind had taken hold of her umbrella and, as she had not let go, had carried her for what, at this length of time, she now considered to be great distances, as far as from cliffs into the sea, but what, as it actually happened, had been no more than three or four feet and into a puddle. "And I said 'Nanny, if I hadn't my egg in my pocket I should have been drowned.'" Julia could now see herself swaying down 10,000 feet tied to a red and yellow parachute. "So you see," she said, "I can't ever leave it behind now, can I?"

"Yes, I must have looked a sight with my skinny legs," and as these were now one of her best features she stretched them out under his nose, "sailing away under my umbrella with the nanny waving so I shouldn't get frightened and let go. I was such a shrimp in those days."

"I bet you never were," he said.

"I was."

"And what about your top?"

"What about my top? Who told you about my top?"

"Nobody."

"Who told you? I've never said a word about it to anyone."

"You must have done or I should not have known," he said uneasily.

Who could have told him? Claire surely wouldn't have. People you trusted talked about you behind your back and ruined everything. He must have been laughing at her all the time she was on about her charms.

"Oh, Max," she said, "you are so tiresome." And then, to cover up her tracks, "First you wouldn't tell me who Embassy Richard's girl was and now you won't say who told you about me. Who is it?"

He made as if to sit on the arm of her chair.

"No," she said, "and if you won't come out with it then you can't expect me to go on filling you up with things to laugh at me about."

"But I was not laughing."

"Very well then, what toys did you have when you were a little boy?"

He thought this was an unlucky business. Rather shamefacedly he said:

"I had a Teddy Bear."

"All little boys have Teddy Bears."

"Well I say, Julia, I can't help that, can I?"

"What else did you have? What did you have you are ashamed of now?"

"But Julia really, what is there to be ashamed of in a wooden egg?"

"Who said I was ashamed? Don't be so ridiculous. Go on now, what did you have?"

He lied and said: "I had a doll as well."

"I don't believe it. What sort of a doll?"

"Well, it was dressed up, a girl, in an Eton blue frock."

"Did you?" she said beginning to smile at last. "And did you take her to bed with you?"

"Of course. I wouldn't sleep without it."

"How sweet," she said ironically, "how perfectly sweet. And are you ashamed of her now?"

"No, why should I be?"

"No," she said, calming down, "there's no reason why one should be, is there?" After all, when one was little one was just like other little boys and girls. But she could not get over someone having told him. Had they been laughing at her over it? Or had he been asking people about her?

"How did you get to know?" she said.

"Someone told me."

"Yes, I know, but how? I mean people don't just tell things like that."

He took the plunge into another lie.

"Well, if you must know," he said, "I asked them."

"Oh, you did, did you? So then you know."

"Know what?"

"The story of my top."

"No, I don't. All I was told was that you had one—'like Julia who keeps a top'—they said."

She left over thinking out whether he had really asked after her until she was alone.

"Oh, is that all you know? Then would you like to hear? You swear you aren't laughing."

"I swear."

"How much would you like to know?"

Again he came over as if to sit on the arm of her chair.

"If you do that," she said getting up, "I shan't be able to tell you about my top."

He thought bother her top.

"And it's most frightfully important."

"Do tell me."

"Do you really want to know? Then I'll tell you. There's no story at all about my top. I've just always had it, that's all."

He advanced on her as if to kiss her.

"No, no," she said, "it's too early in the day yet for that sort of thing," and as he still came forward she began to step back.

"No, Max, I'm not going to start a chase round this squalid room." And as he came up to her she brought her hands smack together as though she were bringing him out of a trance. "Go back and sit in your chair," she said, "mix yourself another drink if you like, but you aren't going to muss me up now." He did as he was told and she was pleased she could make him do as she told him. Then she wondered if he wasn't angry, which he was. So she came over to where he was sitting, and, his hands taken up with pouring out his drink, she kissed his cheek and then sat down opposite.

There was a silence and then he exclaimed:

"By God, I wonder if they have sent up those flowers." He went to telephone and got on to Alex at last and asked him. Alex said yes the flowers had arrived.

"Are they all right? I mean are they decent ones?" Alex said they were and Julia wondered, when he put down the receiver and went over to the window, that he had not asked Alex to have them sent up to her.

In the meantime Hignam had persuaded Robin Adams that he would do better to come upstairs and see what had become of the others. Against his better judgment Mr. Adams had agreed. As he had not been able to leave this hotel owing to those steel doors having been shut down, he considered he might as well be with Angela if he could not get away from their bloody party. He might be able to be of service to her yet.

Now both Julia and Angela had kissed their young men when these had been cross, when Mr. Adams had made off down in the station and when Max had stopped chasing Julia to sit in his chair.

People, in their relations with one another, are continually doing similar things but never for similar reasons.

All this party had known each other for some time, except Max and Angela. Max had taken them up and they had got to know Angela through him. When Max had asked her she had insisted on going although her parents had objected that she did not know them well. Now that she was with them she was not enjoying it because she found she was without what she would call one supporter among them.

For when Angela had kissed Mr. Adams she had not wanted him to stay, it had been no more than a peck, but now she had seen more of their party she wished she had kissed him harder, and she was beginning to blame him. He had been extremely tiresome and he had deserved it when she had sent him off. But she felt now that she had never deserved it when he had gone.

As for Julia she had kissed Max to keep him sweet so to speak, and so, in one way, had Miss Crevy kissed her young man. But what lay behind Julia's peck was this three weeks they both had in front of them, it would never do to start too fast and furious. Angela had no such motive because Mr. Adams was not coming with them.

Angela then was more than missing her young man. Accordingly when he was led by Robert Hignam into this room where she was sitting she was glad to see him. And Alex was very glad to see him. He had been made more and more nervous by Miss Crevy because he could see she was getting in a state. He called out what would he have to drink and Angela said to him:

"Where have you been all this time?"

Now that he did see her again Mr. Adams was so thankful he could find nothing to say. He thought she looked so much more lovely than ever, almost as though he had expected to find she had been assaulted by those others with her clothes torn and her hair hanging down as he put it, although she wore it short. It was then her mood so swiftly changed that it began to seem too tiresome the way he stood there saying nothing when he should have come back long ago. Unfortunately for him he was so taken up with his feeling of how madly beautiful she was that he feared he would give himself away if he went anywhere near her. She felt she could never forgive him if he stayed away, but he went over to Alex and Robert Hignam and mixed himself a drink, turning his back.

If Julia's fears had left her earlier when Max arrived in the lounge downstairs and, at the first sign of him, she had forgotten how angry she had been at his not turning up before, Angela was now the reverse of comforted when she saw Mr. Adams, even if she had been longing for him to come back. Anyway she thought it monstrous that he should stand as he did with his back to her. She said:

"Isn't someone going to ask me what I'd like to drink?" and she put emphasis on the someone. This brought them all over to her side apologizing and carrying the tray with everything on it. When Mr. Adams apologized he tried pathetically enough to make his voice sound as though he were saying in so many words how sorry he was that he had ever gone and even, by the tone of it, how unlucky she was to have one such as he so full of her. But his putting himself in the wrong only made her feel more sure that she was right and he might as well have said it to his glass for she proceeded to ignore him.

Her answer was to begin making up to Alex. She called him darling, which was of no significance except that she had never done so before, and he did not at once tumble to it that her smiles and friendliness for him, which like any other girl she could turn on at will so that it poured pleasantly out in the way water will do out of taps, had no significance either. Still it was very different from how she had been when they were alone together and as he could not bear people being as cross and hurt with him as she had seemed to be he was both surprised and pleased.

"And, darling," she said to Alex, "do you know what is on the other side of that door there?"

He went to see. "Beds!" he cried.

"Yes, twin beds. But I brought my own sheets."

He was still pleased even if this last remark embarrassed him as much as it had done when, at first sight of him down in the station she had called out had he brought his bed. Then he wondered if this change of manner did not come from her wanting to annoy this Robin Adams or to make him jealous. He said she thought of everything and went on,

"But it's really rather early for that sort of thing, isn't it? There's no close season, I know that, but we've got the whole night before us, if you know what I mean."

"Alex, darling, how can you speak like that? It's the most pansy thing I ever heard you say. And in any case," she went on, "it wouldn't be very nice in a sleeper, would it?" Alex passed this off by saying he had given up all idea of their getting a train that evening. As for Mr. Adams he had been so tormented when he saw her again by such a crawling frenzy of love for her that he had not been fit to hear what was going on. This now, however, began to percolate through to him as when clouds curtain an August day that has been enormously still and soft with elms swooning in the haze; and as hot days can become ominous and dark so soon he began to dread what she might make him hear.

Alex said well come along then, knowing that she would never commit herself in front of those others. He suspected that she was only trying to distress this poor creature Adams and was curious to see how she would get out of going into that bedroom with him. He was sure she would never do it and yet she would only make herself look ridiculous now if she did not go. She said he didn't seem very keen, it was hardly flattering to her she said and he thought of answering this by asking her why didn't she try one of the others then, but he refrained, he was afraid this would be too awkward for her. All he did say was that she would soon see who was being flattered once the door was locked on them.

This surprised her into saying, "Oh, I don't think I'd allow you to do that." Her pretence was wearing rather thin he thought and decided to drive her further into a corner. He asked why on earth not and was enormously touched when she explained that she would never let him lock the door because of course she would not mind being caught with him. He suspected she was only playing him up and he knew it was fatuous but he could not help being flattered. He tried to appear cross in order to hide this and so as to lead her on.

"You mean it would not matter if you were caught with me, either to you or anyone else," he said. Robert Hignam interrupted:

"Don't let that worry you. I'll stand on guard and if I whistle three times, what, you'll know someone is coming."

Mr. Adams walked to the window and wondered, as he tried not to hear, if he was going to be sick.

"But I don't mind," she said, "you old silly," using one of Claire's expressions to her husband, "don't you understand I don't mind if anyone did find us? Has no one ever made a proposal to you?"

This word proposal seemed to him to have a fatal ring and rather in desperation he said well, all right, come on then. "Well, all right, come on then," she echoed, "that's a fine way to put it. Well, hold the door open for me."

"Where on earth is Max?" said Mr. Adams, turning round from his window. Alex and Robert Hignam were disgusted to see his face had gone white.

"Now, look here, Angela," Alex said, determined now to escape, "what about that hotel detective?"

Robert Hignam led Mr. Adams away to have a drink in the other corner.

"I must say you don't seem very gallant," she said and thought poor Robin had looked awful, but he must learn his lesson and it was too late to turn back now, she would look silly if she did.

"Alex," she said, "Alex," and jerked her head towards that other room she stood outside by the open door. He saw now those others were not watching, that she only wanted to say something in private and he felt proportionately foolish for ever having imagined she meant a rough and tumble. He hurried in and she shut them in and said:

"Now you must go straight out into the corridor by that other door over there and don't come back."

"You aren't going to do something awful, are you?" he said, because after all he did not know her well enough to say he would stand for no further baiting of Mr. Adams.

"Now, Alex, run along now at once," and he did go, feeling outraged at having been so used. The moment he had shut the door she clapped her hands twice. Mr. Adams, of course, was in her room at once, slamming the door behind him so Robert Hignam could not follow. He found her sitting in front of the glass, powdering her face, and apparently calm as calm.

"What?" he said, "what?"

"What do you mean?" she said.

"Was that you slapping someone's face?" he said and he was panting hard.

"Who slapped whose face? I didn't hear anyone," she said.

"I heard it twice," he said and his knees were trembling.

She burst into tears, her face screwed up and got red and she held her handkerchief to her nose and sniffled as if that was where her tears were coming from.

"Oh, my God," he said and then his knees went so that he thought he would sink to the floor, where he had been standing.

Speaking through her handkerchief, her voice going up and down and interrupted by sobs, grunts and once she choked, she was saying:

"You've been so beastly to me. Going away when you did. As if I was nothing to you. And all these beastly people being beastly to me.

How do you expect me to love you? How could you go like that? Oh, I do feel so miserable." At this point she got hiccups. "How could you? I feel I could die. I feel so miserable."

He began moving towards her, saying darling, darling. By this time they neither of them knew what they were doing.

When Alex came back through the corridor into this sitting room where they had all been, Robert Hignam became facetious which was his way of hiding curiosity.

"I say, old boy, that was a bit sudden, wasn't it, what did you do to the girl?"

Alex hated him for it. He said if he could only strangle her now he would, "and you too," he thought of saying.

"But come on, what did you do to the poor girl to make her fetch you one like that?"

"Nothing, you poor fool, nothing at all. Oh, all right, laugh, yes, but can't you see all she was doing was playing me up to make her boy friend."

Robert felt somehow he had been put in the wrong, but he was not going to stop for that, he wanted to get down to it. "Right," he said, "right, I'd spotted that. As a matter of fact, if I'd been you I doubt if I'd have gone in the first place."

"Afraid of Claire coming in I suppose."

"Here, lay off. But all's well that ends well I expect, isn't it?" he said, nodding to the bedroom door and getting to it.

"You silly idiot, Bob, she's probably putting him through a hoop in some fabulous way."

"I don't know, he's probably got all he wanted by now, but I wouldn't stand for her slapping me for it." He waited till he saw there was no more to come and then he said he wondered what the others were doing.

Claire was sitting telephoning in the room outside Miss Fellowes' bedroom with Evelyn Henderson telephoning too; for some reason this room had two telephones. The door between had been cruelly left open so that her aunt, if her condition was so she could hear, could do so. Both Claire and Evelyn then were speaking at one and the same time and Claire was saying:

"Yes, Mrs. Knight, she is sleeping now." Mrs. Knight was maid to Miss Fellowes. "I don't think you need worry too much about her. No, you would never be able to get here, I shouldn't come along if I were you. No, Mrs. Knight, you mustn't. For one thing the traffic simply isn't running, you would never get here, and then if you did you would never be able to get in, we are simply in a state of siege you know, yes, no one's allowed in or out. Yes, nanny and her friend are with us, they have been angels. Of course, I had a terrible time getting her up here, she had to be carried."

Miss Henderson was telephoning to a female friend.

"My dear," she said, "you would hardly believe it but you remember I told you I was going to the South of France, I'd been looking forward to it so much for such a long time. The fact is that with this fog no trains are running and I've a very good idea, though I've said nothing to the others about it, that we shan't get away at all. Well, the difficult part of it is that I've closed my little flat up you see and sent the woman who looks after me away on her own holiday. Mrs. Jukes, yes. What's that? My dear, do you really mean it, that would be kind of you. May I really? It would only be for one night at the most. You will put me up, you're sure it won't be too much of a bother? My dear, that is too kind of you. Several extraordinary things have happened I can't tell you about now. What's that?"

Claire was saying:

"Now, Mrs. Knight, you're not to worry like this. Of course I don't know what would have become of her if I hadn't been here. No, we don't know what the matter with her is yet. The doctor said a rest would put everything right and after all we must take what the doctors say, mustn't we? Of course, I have given her a hot water bottle. Well, it's her breathing, so short you know. Has she ever had anything of this kind before?"

Evelyna was still talking:

"I can't tell you the name now," she said, almost whispering into the receiver, "but the doctor says she is drunk. No, don't laugh because I think she is very ill indeed. It's not extremely nice. My dear, she had a pigeon, all wet, done up in brown paper. Well, yes wet. I think it's some sort of a sexual fit, don't you agree? With women of her age, yes, she is just that age, it so often is, don't you think? What I am so concerned about is whether it won't come out in another and more violent form, do you see what I mean?"

"No, Mrs. Knight," Claire was saying, "of course it's all very unpleasant for me you know, there have been certain things that really have been—well I won't go on, no, I won't tell you now they would only bother you, but I've made arrangements to get an ambulance directly they can bring one round to send her back to you. Oh, not at all. Poor Auntie May. Good-bye."

Her Auntie May was going over her row with that girl in the bar. Very white she lay still as death on her back and her lips moved, only she had no voice to speak with. Well, she was saying, if there's no one to serve me I might just as well not be here at all. And a voice spoke soundless in answer through her lips. It said everyone must wait their turn. She replied she had waited her turn and that people who had come after had been served first.

It might have been an argument with death. And so it went on, reproaches, insults, threats to report and curiously enough it was mixed up in her mind with thoughts of dying and she asked herself whom she could report death to. And another voice asked her why had she brought a pigeon, was it right to order whisky, did she think, when she was carrying such a parcel? And she did feel frightfully ill and weighed down, so under water, so gasping. It was coming on her again. And she argued why shouldn't she order whisky if they always had it when they were children, and as for the pigeon it was saving the street-cleaner trouble, when they died they were never left out to rot in the streets nowadays. But the voice asked why she had washed it and she felt like when she was very small and had a dirty dress. She said out loud so that she frightened those nannies. "Oh, why can't you leave me alone?" She struggled to turn over on her side but when they both laid their hands to soothe her then she felt them to be angels' hands and had some rest.

But there was nothing of that kind for Mr. Adams. As Alex had guessed, he was being put through the hoop. It was a malign comedy Miss Crevy was creating as she acted.

"But how could I tell," he was saying and he was by her side now while she watched his back in a mirror behind him, "how could I tell how much you minded?"

"If you had cared for me you would," she said.

"You know I do."

"But how do you show it, by going off just when I need you most?"

"Yes, but darling, you told me to go."

"My dear," she said, "that was only because you had been so beastly to me."

"I thought you wanted to go with these people and that you didn't want me."

For one moment she thought she felt so she might burst into tears again and admit she did not want to go, but then it struck her that he would insist on her coming away if she said it. What she wanted to do was to make him properly sorry that she was going, so she said:

"How do you expect me to love you if you don't respect my feelings?"

He felt as though he was gazing into a prism, and he could see no end to it.

"But, my darling, I do, you must believe me, I do."

"And how do you show it?" she asked. "As soon as I'm a little bit upset you go off as if I was being difficult or something."

"But you told me to go."

"You'd been so rude about Claire Hignam's aunt."

"I'm afraid I was very rude about her and I hope you will believe me when I say how very sorry I am if anything I said was rude about her."

"I never wanted you to go, you see," she said.

"Oh, God," he said, reaching depths he had never known about before, "I wish I was more worthy of you. When I think how wonderful you are from the top of your wonderful golden head to your toes."

"Is it gold?" she said, putting her hands up to it.

"It is," he said and coming to sit by her on the stool in front of that looking glass he lightly kissed the hair above her ear. As he did this he looked into the glass to see himself doing it because he was in that state when he thought it incredible that he should be so lucky to be kissing someone so marvellous. Unluckily for him she saw this in the mirror she had been watching his back in. She did not like it. She got up. She said:

"I won't have you watching yourself in the mirror when you're kissing me. It proves you don't love me and anyway no nice person does that."

"Darling," he said, "are you being reasonable?"

"It's not a question of being reasonable. The fact is you despise me. You think I'm too easy, you treat me like a tart."

He lost his temper. "I won't have you say things like that," he said, "you torture me, I'm in such a condition now I don't know what I'm doing. And I've been like that for the past year." Then it seemed monstrous to him that he should speak to her in anger. "I don't mean it," he said. "I don't know what I'm saying."

"Will you promise never to leave me again like that?"

"I promise."

"Well then," she said smiling directly at him, "I expect I have been unreasonable as you call it."

"You haven't," he said stoutly.

"Yes, I expect I have. But you see it's different with women. I expect I have been being tiresome, but in some ways it was too much."

He said: "Do you know what I think is the matter with us, at all events I know it is with me?"

She thought now he is going to talk about getting engaged again.

"No," she said, "what is it?"

"You won't be angry with me."

She knew then it must be what he was going to say.

"No," she said, moving further away from him for safety's sake.

"I don't know how to say it. I bet you know what's coming too."

She thought why couldn't he get on with it and then, looking at him, saw that fatuous smile on his face he always wore on these occasions.

"No," she said.

"Well, really it's that I think we are in an unnatural relationship to each other. You know that I'm in love for ever with you. I know that you don't see this as I do but don't you think that if we could do away with this sort of being at a distance from each other, if we could only tell the world that we were in love by publishing our engagement, don't you feel that it would make things easier for us? I'm not saying this from my point of view. I can't help believing, even if I make you angry with me again, that you do care something for me or else," and he hesitated here, "well here goes, you would not have been as put out as you were when I went off." He went on rather quickly, "I must ask you to believe that I'd never have gone off when I did if I hadn't sincerely thought you wanted me to." In his embarrassment he became even more formal again, "I must ask you to believe that I wouldn't for anything in the world give you a second's unhappiness," and he was going to add because I love you so, but he realized in time he was in such a state he might burst into tears if he said it, so, having lost his thread he wound up by saying, "you must believe that."

There was complete silence. He picked up his argument again.

"I do feel this, I know that if only we were married I could make you feel differently about me."

"My dear," she said, "you've told me that before and I know who said it to you, it was your grandmother, wasn't it? In her generation everybody's marriages were arranged for them and as they were never allowed to be alone with a man for more than three minutes, of course the poor darlings fell for the first man they were left alone with."

He said nothing at all.

"My dear, it is perfectly sweet of you and I think you are sweet too, but you must give me time. You know what you and I both think about marriage, that it's the most serious thing one can do. Well, it's just simply that I can't be sure."

He still said nothing. He was looking at the carpet. From her having to go on talking she became palpably insincere. She was also looking at the carpet. She said:

"You see, I might make you unhappy and you are much too sweet for anyone to risk doing that to. I believe if I saw anyone making you unhappy I would go and scratch their eyes out, yes I would. And so don't you see I can't, I mustn't be in a hurry; you do see, don't you?"

He got up and walked up and down once or twice and then he stopped and asked her did she know how Miss Fellowes was now. He still would not look at any more of her than her toes. She supposed she had been beastly to him again but why, she asked herself, must he choose this hotel room of all places to propose in, with beds slept in by hundreds of fat, middle-aged husbands and wives. And this particular time.

"They are being frightfully mysterious about her," she said.

Almost paralysed by his misery he said:

"Are you sure you wouldn't like some tea?"

"Well, we can't very well, can we?" she said, "Max isn't here. I got some for those two old nannies when I found them crying their eyes out outside about Miss Fellowes, but that was different. Do you know I'm inclined to agree with you that she is being a thorough old nuisance. And then Alex, as I thought, very rudely sent for the drinks there were in that other room, but that's his affair. I don't see very well how we can order tea, do you, without Max?"

"But I'll pay for it on a separate bill."

"You don't know what he's like, he'd never let you and all these others trade on that, I think it's too disgusting."

There was another silence.

"Darling," she said, "don't take all this too tragically. After all I'm only going away for three weeks, and I'm hoping by that time I'll have been able to make up my mind. You do understand?" And as he stood still with his back turned to her she came up and, rather awkwardly, took him by one finger of his sweating hand.

Amabel's flat had been decorated by the same people Max had his flat done by, her furniture was like his, his walls like hers, their chair coverings were alike and even their ash trays were the same. There were in London at this time more than one hundred rooms identical with these. Even what few books there were bore the same titles and these were dummies. But if one said here are two rooms alike in every way so their two owners must have similar tastes like twins, one stood no greater chance of being right than if one were to argue their two minds, their hearts even must beat as one when their books, even if they were only bindings, bore identical titles.

In this way Max and Amabel and their friends baffled that class of person who will judge people by what they read or by the colour of their walls. One had to see that other gross of rooms and know who lived in them to realize how fashionable this style of decoration was, how right for those who were so fashionable, and rich of course, themselves.

If people then who see much of each other come to do their rooms up the same, all one can say is they are like household servants in a prince's service, all in his livery. But in the same way that some footmen will prefer to wear livery because there can then be no question of their having to provide clothes so, by going to the same decorator, these people avoided any sort of trouble over what might bother them, such as doing up their rooms themselves, and by so doing they proclaimed their service to the kind of way they lived or rather to the kind of way they passed their time.

They avoided all discussions on taste and were not encumbered by possessions; what they had was theirs in law but was never personal to them. If their houses were burned down they had only to go to the same man they all thought best to get another built, if they lost anything or even if it was mislaid the few shops they went to would be glad to lend whatever it might be, up to elephants or rhinos, until what had been missed could be replaced.

This role applied to everything they had except themselves, being so rich they could not be bought, so they laid more store than most on mutual relationships. Rich people cling together because the less well off embarrass them and there are not so many available who are rich for one rich man who drops out to be easily replaced.

Again, as between Amabel and Max, as indeed between all of them, there was more, there was her power over him as we shall see which she valued not least because both were so rich, there was also and most important that she found him altogether attractive. Also she did not see why she need let these girls who were after his money have it all their own way while he was paying for them.

She had not taken long to find out where Max was in hiding. When she rang up the airport she had not used her own name to ask if he was there, so they made no difficulty about telling her they had not seen him. She knew with all this fog he would be waiting his first chance to be off and, as she knew him, that he would be entertaining his party, so she began ringing every Terminus Hotel. If he had already been out of England she might not have followed, but now she realized he must be delayed, she really did not see why he should go without her. And this feeling grew until she made out she could not do without him, until, as she thought it over, knowing he was still there, she realized she was lost alone or so it seemed. In this way, where other women might have given him up and consoled themselves, blaming him for his lies, and might have sat down to make up their minds they would let him go because they could not trust him, she found out where he was at once without any trouble and went there.

She told her maid to pack and follow on while she set out on foot. She would save twenty minutes by walking.

She saw nothing of what she passed by, not the crowds of people who had lost their way or those who, faced by such beauty suddenly looming up on them through darkness, had fingered their ties, stepped exaggeratedly to one side, or turned and followed mumbling to themselves.

While she was on her way Angela, still holding on to his finger, had told Adams they must go back or what would those others think of them and still holding on because she felt almost sorry, as she was telling herself it was not his fault, it was the effect she had on him, she led him back. She dropped his finger once they were fairly back in this room. Adams thought to himself these two must know how it is with me, blast them, and that he did not care. He saw, and he thought that proved it, how Alex did not look at either of them, whereas Angela, who had also noticed this, thought it must be that Alex disapproved of what she might have done. She did not care.

Adams went off to mix himself a drink. That's it, she thought to herself, they say they're heartbroken and then they go and drink it off. In any case why take drinks from Max when he says he can't stand him and when he says he won't have anything to do with him. She decided it was selfishness and said to Alex:

"Well and what's happened?"

"Nothing. We've been here, that's all."

Hignam just looked from Adams to Miss Crevy and from Miss Angela Crevy back to Adams.

"Oh, dear," she said and sat down. She looked at her Adams and kept her eyes on him. She began to feel hopeless and asked herself if she had not treated him badly. Usually when she was watching him he knew at once and would look up in hopes her eyes might give him that encouragement they had now and which he had never yet seen, but this time he was too low, doubled up with cramp, he was drowning in his depth. He watched his glass, afraid to show his eyes, and she watched, offering what he wanted. In a moment she looked away, blaming him for not knowing how she felt.

She wondered if they could have heard what had been said and then thought it would have been impossible so long as Alex had not listened through the keyhole, but then she said to herself he would never have done that with Robert Hignam there. Or did men do such things? It was into this strangling silence that Amabel arrived.

She was lovely and when she opened the door and came in they looked up and knew again how beautiful she was.

"Hullo," she said, "at last I've found you."

Robert Hignam was very much surprised to see her. He knew from his wife that Max, if he came at all, would come alone. Alex was surprised for he expected Max would leave her behind. Mr. Adams, when he was introduced by Angela, who barely knew her, had no idea of any complication, to him she was no more than another member of this lot he despised and hated. He did not even admire her. So that when she asked, as she did at once, what Max had done with himself, it was he who answered that he was upstairs with Julia. No one could imagine how he knew.

"I supposed so," she said, giving an appearance of just being late and that she had not bothered to hurry. Alex and Robert Hignam then rushed in, chattering to entertain her and she took this easily, charmingly, though she was rather silent. She made one think she was so used to it all, that it was sweet of them and she liked it, but that she knew a thing worth two of that. They grew almost boisterous offering her chairs and cups of tea and anything they could think of. When they had begun to die down she drew Miss Angela Crevy on one side.

She began to make secrets which was her way when she did not know how things would turn out. Whispering so those others could not hear, she said how nice it was to see Angela. This was very flattering and she went on that Angela must be a dear and do something for her and come to her rescue. She could not be left alone with Max, even for one moment, he had such a temper and would be so cross at her for being late.

Angela warmed to her and said she ought not to fuss, which Amabel had not thought of doing, and that Max had been most frightfully late himself. They had only really found him when they had left the station to come into this hotel she said, and Amabel explained this by claiming that Max had been telephoning her to make haste.

If it hadn't been for the fog, she said, tenderly smiling, she might have missed their train. And Angela believed her when she said all she had been was late and at once assumed she had always been coming. Indeed she had come to think this was another thing the others had been keeping from her.

Amabel by now had had enough of Miss Crevy. "Alex dear," she called out, "come and talk to me. It's so lovely to see you and I did get into such a state when I thought I was going to miss you. I was so very late." He said again he was so glad to see her, and he was glad, but he could not think what it meant her being here and was placidly apprehensive.

"My dear," Amabel went on at him, "I wonder if you would ring down and order me a bath."

"How splendid," he said, "of course."

"I got so dirty coming along. My maid will be up in a minute. Of course it will have to have a room with it and then you can come and talk to me through the door."

It was at this point Mr. Adams left them again, unnoticed now by all, unsung.

"Though," she said, talking a lot for her, "it would be funny if my bathroom was on the corridor and you had to talk from it in front of everyone."

"I couldn't," he said, "it is prowling with detectives. Is that the office? Mr. Adey wants another room with a bath, one of his guests here wants to have one."

When Angela heard him order yet another thing in Max's name she looked guiltily round to see whether Adams had heard. She was relieved to find he was gone for she would have felt worse if it had been said in front of him. On her own as she was now it was different, she did not mind so much, for she did not know any of them at all well; when she had seen Max it had been at night in night clubs when he had usually been with Amabel. And she was so young that having Amabel with them was more exciting for her than Max alone could ever be. Amabel had her own position in London, shop girls in

Northern England knew her name and what she looked like from photographs in illustrated weekly papers, in Hyderabad the colony knew the colour of her walls. So that to be with her was for Angela as much as it might be for a director of the Zoo to be taking his okapi for walks in leading strings for other zoologists to see or, as she herself would have put it, it was being grand with grand people. And if she had been nervous once she was not so any more for she felt Amabel would put them right now that she was here, she would see that Max did not abandon them. She was someone. And Amabel had asked her help so she was in league with her now. In fact her one criticism was that she thought the others were too squalid. Alex dragged them all down the most; it was absurd he could not be natural even about ordering things. It was too much he should make them embarrassed about something elementary and she almost made up her mind to say she would pay herself next time.

"But what about your bath salts?" Alex said just as Claire and Evelyna came in from where they had been telephoning.

"Have I packed mine?" said Claire, alive to every danger, "how enchanting to see you darling," she said to Amabel, wondering why she was here. "Do they let bath salts through the customs free? Is it true there's alcohol in them to freshen up one's skin?" Amabel explained she was going to have a bath, she was asking Alex to ring up her maid to bring her crystals, and Robert Hignam offered her a drink which she refused. She never drank spirits and very little wine, she was serious about her complexion.

Now even Miss Crevy began to notice how more than strained they had become. Alex's voice cracked when Amabel's maid could not understand about her bath salts; he kept on saying yes she is going to have a bath. Evelyn had only just greeted her and this feeling was intensified when Claire began to explain about her Auntie May and how she was so ill.

"We have had the doctor, Robert did you pay him, what does one do about hotel doctors, Amabel, do you know, or do they put it on the bill?" She looked round and saw her husband was not listening, he was staring at Amabel. "Yes," she went on, "it really is too strange, Evelyn and I can't make her out at all, it's so unlike her." And then, more embarrassing still, she realized Amabel was not listening.

"So here we are, my dears," she said at large, "stuck here without..."—our host she was about to say and then thought better of it, it was better not to mention him, it always was. "Without any chance to get away," she made it into and then bit her lip; put that way Amabel might take it they were all here to escape her which of course in one sense they were, but then what could it matter when people were as rude as Amabel.

But it was not rudeness, not positively that in her case. It is true she did not bother but then she did not expect it of others so that it was almost flattering when she did take notice. At any rate Alex was pleasantly surprised when he had put back the receiver to find Amabel thanking him before he had time to let her know her maid was coming round directly. He did not see she had done this to stop the others knowing. But he did get as far as to feel bewildered; for while he had been sure Amabel would not be coming with them he could not be certain. When she had come in so naturally he had been almost ready to believe Max had changed his plans again as only rich people can and do. Now in his conversation with her maid he had found out she had only just made up her mind to come otherwise she would have had her things packed some time ago or anyway have given orders. It might have been that Max telephoned her but that was not likely if Julia had been with him all this time. So he was embarrassed to know what he should do, whether or no he should get word to Max that Amabel was here, as it seemed likely Amabel had come unknown to Max.

And Alex had that shock when one's thought is answered by someone present, so much so he wondered if, without knowing, he had let what he was thinking out. For what he had almost decided was to let things well alone, he had all but made up his mind he did not know enough to interfere by tipping Max the wink. But when he had been thanked for telephoning, and by her, it was so like gratitude for keeping other's secrets and for not doing what he could and should, he had no alternative but to decide that he must warn him.

As for Amabel, she was not going to bother about the others, excepting Alex. Miss Crevy would have been surprised to learn Amabel had spoken to her only to make secrets and because she guessed the other girls would be against her coming, so that it seemed policy to make one friend at once. Also she wanted to make sure she would not be left alone with Max before she had found out how things were. Miss Crevy would have been surprised as well to learn that Amabel classed her equally with the others and lower, and with contempt as being more out for a free trip abroad because she could less afford to go if she was not taken. Amabel was a money snob. So that Amabel's silence, which Angela in her ignorance might call poise, was no more than wariness coloured by distaste for her own sex. She was here to manage Max and was not going to bother with anyone else but Alex.

At the same time no one can be sure they know what others are thinking any more than anyone can say where someone is when they are asleep. And if behind that blank face and closed eyelids and a faint smile on closed lips they are wandering it may be in Tartary, it is their stillness which makes it all possible to one's wildest dreams.

In her silence and in seeming unapproachable, although he realized it might be studied, and Alex admired her so much he was almost jealous of her, it seemed to him she was not unlike ground so high, so remote it had never been broken and that her outward beauty lay in that if any man had marked her with intimacy as one treads on snow, then that trace which would be left could not fail to invest him, whoever he might be, with some part of those unvulgar heights so covered, not so much of that last field of snow before any summit as of a high memory unvisited, and kept.

He realized she always worked on him by being there and this woke him to how embarrassed they all were except for Angela and Amabel. Again he offered chairs and drinks for Claire and Evelyn but he was alone in it this time, Robert was too wary to make any move when he saw his wife was fussed.

"Where on earth have you been, darlings?" Amabel said to them as though they were at fault, and Claire, who no longer wanted to talk about Auntie May in front of her, said "Oh, just outside."

Evelyn Henderson, who was in fact the least well off of all, said to herself why does this woman always make me feel like a schoolgirl.

If people vary at all then it can only be in the impressions they leave on others' minds, and if their turns of phrases are similar and if their rooms are done up by the same firm and, when they are women, if they go to the same shops, what is it makes them different, Evelyna asked herself and then gave the answer: money. Amabel sat there without saying anything; not, so it seemed to Evelyn, because there was anything special about her but because, by being rich or, better still, through having piled up riches in presents from young men, or both, the newspapers had picked her out and now there was no getting away from it, Amabel had grown to be like some beauty spot in Wales. Whether it was pretty or suited to all tastes people would come distances to see it and be satisfied when it lay before them. Amabel had been sanctified, so she thought, by constant printed references as though it was of general concern what she looked like or how beautiful she might be. But then there was no question of beauty here, Evelyn thought, because there were no features, and it could not be called poise, and then she became offensive in her thoughts of her. But Amabel had that azure glance of fame and was secure.

She said: "How on earth did Max ever come to take this awful room?" This was another way to ignore Claire and Evelyn, to talk to them without any mention of what they had been saying and Evelyn, when she found herself agreeing, as she did almost automatically, despised herself for playing up to her. It was a question of prestige, she thought. When you come on a famous view you feel bound to praise it as you do with some famous beauty when you see one. "And I agree with what any well-known lovely says because she is so handsome," she said to herself, "it's not as if I was pretending she was not as beautiful as all that. I have to go and publicly agree with everything she says because she has said it. Really it's craven."

Angela, who had by now forgotten Mr. Adams she was so excited at being, so she thought, in league with Amabel, tried to put in her word for Max as though she had been confided in and was a party to their intimate affairs.

"Oh, no, poor Max," she said, "it's not his fault, every room is like this; of course, I don't know but I expect so."

"Well then," said Amabel, "I bet you had to order drinks," and Alex laughed. "When shall I ever," she went on, "be able to teach him how to make people comfortable," and then was silent.

Claire, who did not care for silences, she thought them unnatural, took up what Amabel had said about this room. While she went rattling on, blaming the directors for allowing decorations such as these and saying she could not think what Julia's uncle was about in letting them do such things, Amabel wondered again how Max would be and what he had on with Julia. She had expected to find him with these others and when she had opened the door she had been braced up to meet him. She was like someone who opens his front door expecting to step out into a gale of wind and then stays bent although he finds he has no wind to lean against, although it is still whining in the chimney and rattling windows. She knew well she could deal with Max but he was always escaping. It was while he was not there that she felt anxious and that was one reason why she had made up her mind to come along.

Mrs. Hignam was still talking. "It is a perfectly ridiculous price to ask for rooms of this kind when you can get something really comfortable for only double at any of the best hotels. I can't understand it," she said and was going on when Amabel, although she had already been told once, expressed what she was feeling:

"Where has Max got to? I've been here fifteen minutes," she said.

Claire thought this was too rude and that anyway they were all sick of this endless thing between Amabel and Max. She would have nothing more to do with it. "Let's go back," she said to Evelyn and when they were outside she said "Well, surely the poor man can call five minutes of his time his own." As they went into Miss Fellowes' room she began to elaborate on this theme. Unaware of her aunt

who had long been unaware of them and of those nannies whose
training made them seem deaf and dumb at moments her voice rose
and fell like a celluloid ball on the water-jet men shoot at and miss at
fairs. When it fell through lack of breath Evelyn, like any paid attendant, put that ball back with an encouraging word and Claire
was off again.

No one answered Amabel and now that he was alone with Angela and her again and that her last remark reminded him he had not
yet got word to Max that she was here, he suddenly felt more strongly
than ever before how these girls were a different species and were
quite definitely hostile. As he looked at them both, exquisitely
dressed, Angela smoking and watching her smoke rings, Amabel
looking at her nails like you and I gaze into crystals, as he looked at
them waiting it struck him again how women always seemed to expect things, and for that matter, events even, to be brought to them
for their pleasure, in white cotton gloves on plates. He determined
he would do nothing, if Max had been in his place he would not
have done anything or even have thought of it, and then it was too
much for these two girls to expect. For he now thought Amabel had
only been late as she had so often been before. He did not see why he
should get Max for her. It was easier to believe her maid had been
mistaken or that she had forgotten her orders to pack the things. In
this way he showed how he had been taken in by Amabel, whose
wish it was that she should not show haste. In this way also he
showed again how impossible it is to tell what others are thinking or
what, in ordinary life, brings people to do what they are doing. So he
sat quiet, said nothing, and watched the bubbles in his glass.

Through those lidded windows, the curtains so thick and heavy
they seemed made of plaster on stage sets, there faintly whispered
through to them in waves of sound as in summer when you are coming on a waterfall through woods and it is still unseen or, in summer,
breathless in the meadows an aeroplane high up drones alternately
loud then soft and low it is so high, what were shouted protests or
cheering or just a hubbub of that crowd away below, all this gently
came in and passed them by. All three wondered and dreaded a little

perhaps in their different ways but no one said anything, there was nothing to say.

Max and Julia, come to an end of talk and speeches, of his saying yes and of her saying no, had moved again to their window upstairs which they had opened and now they were leaning out. The crowds were singing.

Looking down then on thousands of Smiths, thousands of Alberts, hundreds of Marys, woven tight as any office carpet or, more elegantly made, the holy Kaaba soon to set out for Mecca, with some kind of design made out of bookstalls and kiosks seen from above and through one part of that crowd having turned towards those who were singing, thus lightening the dark mass with their pale lozenged faces; observing how this design moved and was alive where in a few lanes or areas people swayed forward or back like a pattern writhing; coughing as fog caught their two throats or perhaps it was smoke from those below who had put on cigarettes or pipes, because tobacco smoke was coming up in drifts; leaning out then, so secure, from their window up above and left by their argument on terms of companionship unalloyed, Julia and Max could not but feel infinitely remote, although at the same time Julia could not fail to be remotely excited at themselves.

When earlier on she had asked him to go down when she had heard someone scream, the crowd was now too great, indeed it was so thick it was plain they could never get out of their hotel to go home if they wanted and she was glad, everything she felt now would come right between them if only it was not hurried, and that promise of the birds which had flown under the arch she stood on would be fulfilled if only, as seemed likely, she could see sea-gulls that night on their crossing. What that promise could be she had no idea, and she did not let herself think of what she wanted, her feeling was just what she had when in a hot bath so exactly right she could not bear to wonder even. In fact she did not want anything different from how things were now this instant. She certainly did not want him to

go down and get in the crowd, although its thousands of troubles
and its discomfort put new heart into her.

"You're not to go down there, even if I ask you," she said rather
loud to him. "No one's to go down there, I tell you."

"What about your servant?"

"Oh, him! Bother him!"

For where she had at one time been nervous and had clutched at
straws to fuss over, she now wanted things to stay as they were and,
if put to it, she would have insisted she had asked Robert to ring the
station master only so as to tease him. Also whatever there is in
crowds had reached into her, for these thousands below were now
working up a kind of boisterous good humour. If they had been angry individually at first at the delay, and at not being able to get in or
out, they were now like sheep with golden tenor voices, so she was
thinking, happily singing their troubles away and being good com-
panions. What she could not tell was that those who were singing
were Welshmen up for a match, and what they sang in Welsh was of
the rape of a Druid's silly daughter under one of Snowdon's wilder
mountains. She thought only they knew what it meant, but it
sounded light-hearted.

Also she felt encouraged and felt safe because they could not by
any chance get up from below; she had seen those doors bolted, and
through being above them by reason of Max having bought their
room and by having money, she saw in what lay below her an exam-
ple of her own way of living because they were underneath and kept
there.

"Aren't you glad you aren't down there?" she said, and he replied
he wondered how it was going to be possible to get them out.

"Have you ever been in a great crowd?" she said, because she had
this feeling she must exchange and share with him.

Down below Amabel broke into their silence by saying:

"Well, and what about my bath, if you please?"

Alex said: "Good Lord, yes, haven't they done anything about it
yet?" apologized, and telephoned down while Angela dutifully made
comments on how impossible it was to get things done in hotels.

Alex was told there was a bath to their room, it was through the bedroom and he passed this news on, and also that her maid was coming.

When she came in she said at once, as though she was alone with Amabel: "Oh, Madam, I had such a time, you would hardly credit it, Madam, but we got here in the car although one man did get up on the running-boards. Oh, Moddom, you can't have any idea of what it's like. Do you think it's the revolution, Madam, and I have your bath-salts unpacked and your bath is ready for you now."

"Shall I come with you and watch you have it?" Angela asked her, but Amabel was not having that.

"Darling," she said, "look, I've something I must say to Alex."

As they went out and Angela was left, wishing once more her Adams was back with her again, she wondered if Amabel was going to let him see her in her bath. But surely not in front of her maid, she thought, without noticing how this would make it better in one sense, even if it could not make it right. After all, she knew them so little, she only knew Amabel as being very smart, but she had not bargained to let Alex see her in her own bath, or any other young man like that, or any man at all, and she hoped she would not have to, not for Max or anyone; it could not be expected of her. And how could Alex make compliments on how Amabel looked in a bath with her maid standing by handing her sponges, or would he make no compliments because it had happened so often before and was so ordinary? She made up her mind she would show what she thought by not going in when Amabel sent for her, and in any case she felt she never would be able to if Alex was there; she could not be by the bath in front of Alex, looking into his eyes it would be as if they had done murder, or so it seemed to her it would be to look into his eyes laid upon the woman's nakedness.

Actually most elaborate precautions were taken, and of this Angela knew nothing because she could not bring herself to go and see. Alex had to stand far away when her maid came out, which she did so continually that Amabel might have been in the way of being brought to bed. He saw nothing of her and did not even hear her well.

Amabel giggled. "She thinks we are in here together," she said, as if she could dream of it, with Alex of all men.

"I know," he said back through her door. And he for his part imagined her where she lay, pink with warmth and wrapped round with steam so comfortable she would be more animated now, more cheerful. Aromatic steam as well from her bath salts so that if her maid had been a negress then Amabel's eyes might have shone like two humming birds in the tropic airs she glistened in.

"Oh, Toddy," she said to her maid, "you have brought the right bath-salts."

"What's that?" he shouted.

She kicked her legs and splashed and sent fountains of water up among the wreaths of sweet steam, and her hands with rings still on her fingers were water-lilies done in rubies.

"Do you take your rings off," he shouted, "when you have your bath?"

"Why?" she said.

"I was wondering what you looked like."

"Sweet of you," she shouted back, and she would have been offended if he had not said something of that kind. She did not think it sweet of him at all.

"Did they make you wear a nightdress in your bath when you were at school?"

She laughed and said he must not shout so loud or Angela would know he was not in with her. Her maid, stifling, wondered if it would not bring her asthma on again.

Auntie May's room was next door and Claire said to Evelyn, Amabel was keeping Alex hanging on. Even those who went to bed with her never were allowed to see her with no clothes on, because someone quite early in her life had carved his initials low on her back with an electric-light wire, or so Embassy Richard had told her.

"D'you think Angela Crevy ever's met him?"

"No I don't," Evelyn said to her. "She's trying to be one of us."

At this poor Auntie May shifted slightly in her bed.

"My dear, what are we to do with her?" Evelyn put a finger to her lips, but Claire went on. "I don't care," she said, "she must get well, it's too absurd her being ill here, letting that idiot doctor say fantastic things about her, even if they might be true. Why are the old allowed to go about alone; they ought to make a law about it. What would have happened to her if we had not been there and Max, he is so perfectly sweet, hadn't taken this room? But it's unfair to him if she doesn't get well soon or get over it, whichever it is, or both," she said.

And Auntie May, half-way round from another spell of what had come over her and struck her down into nightmares and exhaustion and wandering so that she had been diagnosed as tight, and tight she was with dreams spoke up from mists which wrapped her round not sweet and warm. She mistook her niece for another barmaid, and said in a high wavering voice:

"I'm surprised at you, surprised I am," she said, "you should be glad I came in and gave you custom, a customer I came in, that's what you are here for, here for," she said, and was silent. "I shall complain," she said, trying to raise herself on her arm, and Claire leaned forward and said: "Hush, auntie, you don't know what you are saying." This silenced her again.

"Claire, d'you suppose she heard us?"

"What on earth do you mean? My dear, she is raving. Oh, why did she come to be such a worry to us, isn't it a shame?"

"You mean she thought she was talking to a waitress," Evelyn said. "But you know it is so dangerous to speak in front of people when they are ill, you think they can't hear, but one can never tell. I remember my mother telling me when Grannie died the nurse said she had only so long to live, ten hours, or whatever it was then, and she said, 'Don't,' just like that. And that was after she had lain there like a log for two days and nights."

"Well then," Claire whispered, "don't talk in front of her."

"Oh," said Evelyn, also in whispers now, "but she is not going to die, is she?"

"My dear, don't you of all people go and let me down. I've trouble enough on my hands now in all conscience without—oh well," she said, "I'm sorry, it's not easy just now, is it? And where's that wretched husband of mine, why doesn't he do something?"

"But surely that's just it," said Evelyn, "there's nothing to do."

Thomson, who was still looking after Julia's luggage where it had been left until it could be registered, felt he must stretch his legs again. He said to her porter: "Jack, I'll be back," and came out from behind her barricade of trunks to find Edwards sitting on one of Max's suit-cases.

"Mr. Adey, I believe," he said, and raised his hat.

"Mr. Livingstone, I presume, Miss Wray," said Edwards. They both of them laughed. Thomson sat down on yet another pigskin case and said what game was it this they were playing? and he got his answer, hide and seek. Oranges and lemons he suggested was more likely, but no, said Edwards, sardines was all the rage now not blind bloody man's buff, which was kept for Dartmoor Sunday afternoons. Both laughed again.

"Well," Thomson said, "it was a funny game whatever it was, and even if it had not got a name, it was more like drivers waiting outside shops or at dances." He asked if Edwards had had his tea. Neither had so much as tasted it this afternoon. Edwards had some chocolate in bars which he called iron rations, but he explained he did not want to touch that, not knowing but what they might be here all night when they might want something more urgent, for even if it had been three hours or more since their dinner it might be long night before they saw supper. Thomson said he was not going to wait all that long time, and Edwards asked him why he did not go along and see if he could get himself something. Thomson explained it did not taste like it should if he had his tea alone, he liked company with it, and why didn't Edwards come along and see what they could find? But Edwards considered they would find every tea place full. Also he would not leave this dressing-case of his.

"Then what's in it?"

"It's fitted."

"What, gold and silver stoppers and all that? Come on, it's insured and chances are he'd like a new one."

"Go on if you like and pick up some bird, alive or dead, Thomson, and get yourself your cup o' tea if you feel like it."

"What d'you mean, alive or dead?"

"Not but you'll find everything full and more than full out there. There's trouble enough to get in without trying for a cup o'tea. Alive or dead? I meant nothing."

"Not wrapped up in brown paper you didn't?"

"What's that?"

"Oh, nothing. This is a rum thing this party. And they call it pleasure, eh?"

"I don't know. It's not their business if fog comes down like it's done, they can't be accountable for that."

"No, but then why stay here or in that hotel, why not go back and sit down to a nice tea while you wait?"

"It's plain to see you haven't been outside, my lad, not lately. You couldn't get back now if you tried."

"Oh, look at those blue eyes," Thomson said, and Mr. Adey's porter lifted his heavy head. Round one massive up-ended cabin trunk a girl was looking. "Lovely blue eyes, and I like that nose."

Edwards said: "Now then, don't let's have anything like that here."

"Anything?" said Thomson. "Did you 'ear what that rude man called it, a lovely kiss?" he said, still sitting where he did. "What a thing to call it. Listen, if that gentleman with the luggage will drop off again like he 'as been doing this last thirty minutes and my pal here turns his dirty disapproving face, will you give us a kiss, darling? There's none could see with these bags and things."

"I like your cheek," she said scornfully. "Here," she said, "if you want one," and crept round and kissed him on his mouth. Not believing his luck he put his arms round her and the porter said, "God bless me," when a voice over that barricade began calling: "Emily, where are you, Emily?" and he let her go, and off she went.

"God bless 'er little 'eart," the porter said, smacking his lips. He called out to his mate, having to shout it there was so much noise: "Come up out of the bloody ground, and gave him a great bloody kiss when he asked her."

"Poor Thomson," Julia said just then to Max, putting on her hat again, "d'you think he's all right, and what about his tea?"

"We ought to go down," he said.

"Yes, the others will be wondering what's become of us." And what had become of both of them, she asked herself, suddenly despairing; nothing, alas!

"Oh, Max," she said, "everything is going to be all right, isn't it?"

"All right?"

"Do you see, I'm wondering about this journey. All the fog and all that," she said, leading him off.

"You do think our train will run, don't you?" she went on.

"It'll have to."

"I know," she said, "but things don't always go right because they have to. I wonder if I ought to ring my uncle and let him know what's become of us," she said, because she was not and could not be sure Max would come to anything in the South of France. "D'you think I'd better. Max darling, do say something. What do you think?"

He looked at the telephone and considered and at last he told her he saw no point in doing so. And now she remembered those two birds which had flown under the arch she had been on when she had started, and now she forgot they were sea-gulls and thought they had been doves and so was comforted.

"Good heavens! Come along, what will they think?" she said brightening. "We must get on down."

"Well," said Thomson, "and what do you think of that Emily? Emily," he cried in a falsetto voice echoing the old lady who had called her back, but not so loud that she could hear. "Where are you Emily, my lovey-dove?"

"Disgusting, I call it."

"And what's disgusting? Lord, what's in a kiss? It don't mean nothing to her, nor anything to me, but it did make an amount of difference when I hadn't 'ad my tea."

"You do meet some funny ones about these days," Edwards said to the porter. "Still thinking along of his tea and look what he's just got."

"No," said Thomson. "No, it's fellow feeling, that's what I like about it. Without so much as a by your leave when she sees someone hankering after a bit of comfort, God bless 'er, she gives it him, not like some little bitches I could name," he darkly said, looking up and over to where their hotel room would be. Their porter tapped his forehead. "It's been too much for 'im," he cried at large, "too much by a long chalk. So it is for most of these young fellers, carried away by it," he said.

"Waiting about in basements, with no light and in the damp and dark," Mr. Thomson muttered to himself, and if he and that girl had been alone together, in between kisses he would have pitied both of them clinging together on dim whirling waters.

"Well, there you are," said Julia as she came in and before she could see who was there and in such a tone she might as well have been asking where had they all been all this time. "Why it's you, Angela, my dear," she said. "Where are the others?"

"Alex is helping Amabel, actually, in her bath," Miss Crevy said, and wished she had a periscope to see that bomb explode. But if it went off it did so out of sight, for Julia did no more than turn to Max, though she did this in the direction her heart had turned over when she heard.

"How did she get there?" he said, and he felt shocked.

"She walked, she told me, and she got here in front of her maid who came in the car."

"Is Toddy here then?"

"Oh, Max," said Miss Crevy, "who ever heard of Amabel travelling without her maid?"

So she is coming after all, Julia thought, maid and all and six cabin trunks full of every kind of lovely dress. But how unfair, she thought, how vile of her when she knew Max did not want her, how low to pursue him in this way. She also noticed Miss Crevy seemed quick in using her Christian name and wondered if they mightn't somehow be in league. But it was going to ruin their entire trip her coming, and she went over in her mind when she heard him say he had asked Amabel.

She had been wearing her blue dress and the new shoes and they had gone on together alone somewhere to dance and she had been nervous about whether he would have too much to drink perhaps, but anyway it had been fun and lots of people there and then Embassy Richard had come up. How absurd of Angela to call him Embassy Dick like any bird; she was too free the way she made out she knew people. Perhaps that was why Max had seemed so much against him, but when Richard had come up he had said something jokingly about his knowing someone Max was going to leave behind and who would be simply furious at being left. And that was all, come to think of it, and she had taken it to mean Amabel, but she might be wrong, there might be someone else. What could it mean?

"I didn't know Amabel was coming," she said, meaning why had he not told her.

"She was most awfully upset she was so late," Miss Crevy told Max, "she told me to say to you how dreadfully sorry she was, and of course she would have missed the train if it hadn't been for this fog. But you see it was just that, the fog's so thick she simply could not get here, so she says you mustn't be too hard on her, please, she could not really help herself."

Julia said, well anyway they had all got here in time, and that she had no maid to pack for her. "In fact," she said, because this news had upset her so she had to speak about herself, "Jemima the old thing who packs for me, you can't call her a maid really, never can learn to put in my charms. You know," she said to Angela very seriously, "I simply can't go anywhere without them, the most frightful things have happened if I haven't brought them, and not to me only, but to everyone who was with me too. So you see it makes me most terribly nervous. You see I don't know to this minute whether I have them with me or not, and nervous not only for myself but for all of you, my poor darlings."

Miss Crevy did not take this well as she could not understand the calm with which they seemed to accept, not Amabel's presence, which she thought natural, but the fact that Alex was in there with her. It made her furious they should make so little of it, and she burst out:

"Oh, no, but I think it's disgusting his being in there helping with her bath."

This was so sudden it made Julia forget about her charms.

"My dear," she said, "what do you mean, helping?" And Angela who, as soon as she began to explain, felt in some way she was weakening her argument, had to say she did not know how he was helping, and at that she laughed, but he was in there and he ought not to in front of all of them.

"He is not," said Max. Miss Crevy looked to see if he was jealous, but saw that he simply did not believe her.

"But I tell you I heard them."

"My dear, what did you hear about them?" Julia said.

Feeling in some way she was making her argument still weaker Miss Crevy explained how Amabel had asked him in front of her not half an hour ago.

"She did not," said Max, and Miss Crevy said no more. If they did not believe her then let them find out for themselves and then, rather late, it came over her that she had not seen for herself, it was possible Alex was still in the bedroom and she felt foolish until she thought, well anyway if he wasn't in there now he soon would be.

On this Julia left them. She thought Miss Crevy an impossible girl and went to find Claire and Evelyn to tell them and ask after Miss Fellowes. This would be her way of apologizing for having gone off with Max. And Max, who wanted time to face up to this news began to make it by asking Angela if she had all she wanted. She would hardly answer him.

When Julia went into that bedroom where Miss Fellowes lay, she said to Evelyn and Claire, "Well there you are," in such tones she might have been telling them how hard it had been for her to find them, and as though she were saying she had been looking for them all that time she had been upstairs with Max. She asked after Miss

Fellowes and they replied, all this in whispers, and then so soon as she decently could she said would they not leave Miss Fellowes to those nannies, she had something she must tell them. Both wondered if she were going to announce her engagement, but it seemed she was more angry than pleased, and for one moment Claire wondered if that idiot Robert, her idiotic husband, had tried to pounce on her.

When those nannies had been got in and they themselves were in the corridor outside, Julia began on Angela. "Children," she went on, using this word because Evelyn who was older than any of them always used it when she wanted their attention, "what do you think of Angela Crevy? And do you know what she has just accused my darling Alex of? Why of being with Amabel in her bath." At this Claire and Evelyn registered disgust. "Oh, my darlings," she went on, "isn't it too despairing, why must Max out of pure good nature ask people like her to come with his oldest friends who have known each other for ages?" "I know," they both murmured back. "And Amabel, what is she doing, and anyway, why can't that great ninny Angela see she is trying to set us by the ears?"

"Isn't that just what I was saying to you?" Claire said to Evelyn.

"Yes, we were," said Evelyn.

At this they stood all three facing each other with serious faces, when Robert turned the corner and came down that corridor towards them.

"What's this?" he says, "in a committee meeting?" He smells faintly of whisky.

"Go away," says Claire to him, "we're busy. Run along now," she said, and as he went and was just opening the door to go in to Max and Angela, and as they stayed silent so that Max should not hear anything through that open door, the man who had followed Miss Fellowes and whom Alex had taken for a detective also came round that same corner and made after Robert. Julia whispered: "Oh dear, who's this? What can he want?" she said as he went in after Mr. Hignam, "or is it another friend of Max's we have to do with?"

Max, when he saw Hignam, thought it would be best to find out what he could about Amabel rather than pretend he had always known she would be coming, for there was no knowing what she might have said while she was alone with them, so he asked him, "What's this about Amabel?" Miss Crevy took this to mean that Max had believed her when she had, so she thought, told on Alex. But Mr. Hignam had no time to reply that he knew nothing before that false detective was on to him. Putting his head inside he said, "I want you," in educated accents this time.

"Yes," said Robert, taken aback. "Well, what for? Right you are, I'll come outside," he said.

They walked up that corridor where his wife and those two others could not hear them and then Mr. Hignam asked again what might be wanted of him.

"How is she?"

"How's who? My aunt, you mean? I say, who are you?"

"She were mortal bad I reckon when I see her took upstairs," this strange man said, speaking now in Brummagem. "Now don't misunderstand me," he said. "I don't mean any harm, just a civil inquiry, that's all. You see I was sitting nigh her when she was taken bad," and by now he was speaking ordinarily, "and I think I'll just ask after her."

"She's better, thank you," Robert answered, and began to see how he could use this man.

"Well, 'ere's a to-do if you like with this fog and none being able to get off to their own fireside like with no trains running on account of it. But I'm right glad to 'ear from you as she's better. Of course it's different for the likes of you as can afford it, and thank God for it, I say. I'm not one of those as 'olds there ought only to be the poor and no rich in this world, but it's different for you so it is as can take rooms and be a bit comfortable like instead of 'aving to stand like cattle waiting to be butchered in that yard beneath. Not but what I thought," he said going back to Miss Fellowes, "she looked terrible ill down there in that tea-room where I was just getting a bit of comfort down inside me. I remember it now," he said, smacking his lips.

"What did she have down there?"

"Why, bless my soul, not more than one small whisky on account of 'ow strange she was feeling, I'll be bound. The properest lady that ever stepped," he added. "I felt sorry for her, that I did; aye and I thought to myself, my lad, I thought, you can go and ask after her, you know a real lady when you sees one. She's a goner."

"She's what?"

"Oh, aye, she's a goner. She's your aunt, you said. Yes, I don't give her long."

"You know better than the doctor then."

"Aye she's a goner."

"Look here, you doing anything just now, what? I mean if I slipped you ten bob, could you get outside?"

"What for?"

"Ten bob."

"No, what d'you want me to do?" he said in his educated voice again.

"Only to go out and find Miss Julia Wray's man who's called Thomson and ask him if her luggage is all right. He ought to be with it down in that place where it's registered."

After some difficulty Robert got him off and went back to be with Angela and Max. Before he could reach their room Julia called out to him and asked who had that man been and what did he want. Robert answered he had sent him out to find Thomson as she seemed so upset about her luggage, and as he said it he showed how pleased he was; he thought he was killing two birds with one stone. And as he went in and Angela began to ask him this same question, Julia said how perfectly sweet of Robert, and then added to herself, but not that man, couldn't he have gone himself, not that man of all men? She looked so distracted, Claire said to her: "Now, darling, don't get in a fuss."

When Mr. Hignam had explained, Angela said: "But you can't treat him like that, he's the hotel detective."

"He's not."

"But, Robert, I tell you he is," she said, using his Christian name for the first time. "Alex found that out when he came in before, and I was here."

"He isn't one."

This she could take from Max but not from Robert. "How do you know he isn't one?" she said, going white under her make-up. All of a sudden she was so angry she began to tremble from her toes up.

And Amabel was just drying hers on a towel. The walls were made of looking-glass, and were clouded over with steam; from them her body was reflected in a faint pink mass. She leaned over and traced her name Amabel in that steam and that pink mass loomed up to meet her in the flesh and looked through bright at her through the letters of her name. She bent down to look at her eyes in the A her name began with, and as she gazed at them steam or her breath dulled her reflection and the blue her eyes were went out or faded.

She rubbed with the palm of her hand, and now she could see all her face. She always thought it more beautiful than anything she had ever seen, and when she looked at herself it was as though the two of them would never meet again, it was to bid farewell; and at the last she always smiled, and she did so this time as it was clouding over, tenderly smiled as you might say good-bye, my darling darling.

Angela's raised voice came through to her.

"She sounds cross," she said to Alex, and he replied she was cross by nature, she did such dreadful things. "It was too intolerable," he told her, "there was this young man of hers, he had gone before you came, and she left him outside and made me come in where I am now, sent me out again into that corridor and then clapped her hands as though she was slapping my face."

"Oh, no!"

"Yes, it's true."

"Alex, my dear, how very funny. Wasn't it a bit hard on you?" she said to humour him, and went on drying herself. Her bath-towel was huge and she slowly rubbed every inch of herself with it as though she were polishing. She was gradually changing colour, where she was dry was going back to white; for instance, her face was dead white but her neck was red. She was polishing her shoulders now and her neck was paling from red into pink and then suddenly it would go white. And all this time she dried herself she moved her toes as if she was moulding something.

When Alex came to an end she had not properly heard what he had been saying so she said something almost under her breath, or so low that he in his turn should not catch what she had said, but so that it would be enough to tell him she was listening.

As she went over herself with her towel it was plain that she loved her own shape and skin. When she dried her breasts she wiped them with as much care as she would puppies after she had given them their bath, smiling all the time. But her stomach she wiped unsmiling upwards to make it thin. When she came to dry her legs she hissed like grooms do. And as she got herself dry that steam began to go off the mirror walls so that as she got white again more and more of herself began to be reflected.

She stood out as though so much health, such abundance and happiness should have never clothes to hide it. Indeed she looked as though she were alone in the world she was so good, and so good that she looked mild, which she was not.

She put out her tongue and carefully examined this. Then she smiled herself good-bye again and began to powder all over her.

"What on earth are you doing?" he said. "I don't believe you listened to a word I said."

"Is Max out there, d'you suppose?"

"I don't know. Shall I go and find him?"

"No, of course not. Let him find me."

"As you are? In or out of your bath?"

"No such luck for him," she said, and laughed. She began whistling.

Max said he would ask Alex what he thought this man had been, it seemed to him a natural excuse to see what they were doing. Going in he found Alex wearily leaning his shoulder against the shut door of that bathroom.

"Hullo, old boy!"

"Amabel," said Max.

"Why, hullo, darling," she said. "I'm having a bath."

"Good," he said.

Angela came in. "Alex," she said, "didn't you say that man was the hotel detective?"

"What man?"

"The man you gave a drink to."

"I thought he might be, but I shouldn't think so."

He could not have been, for now that he was trying to get out of this hotel, and it was like trying to get out of one world into another, no one in authority seemed to know him. If they let people out they said then they would have to allow them in, they had experienced that before when everything had been broken up, no, he could not go outside. Then he asked them what right they had to keep him in, and they told him it was to protect their own property. He had said he must go out, and then each of those officials had left him.

In the lounge where he was now it was even fuller than it had been. Every seat was occupied and people sat about on their bags as they had done outside when there had been room to sit down. One wall had windows high up along it which looked out over the station, and on their outside ledges were perched young men, mostly amusing themselves at the guests inside. These youths were putting out their yellow tongues at one old lady seated by him, and while he thought how he could get out he watched her shake her paper at them. As he always interfered he told her not to bother, and in this he was right, as she encouraged them by showing temper. But she would not listen. "Go away," she said, and once she had said that began mouthing soundlessly, go away, articulating with her lips at those youths behind glass. They caught on to this and mouthed back through the shut window, only what they brought soundless out were obscenities. He could read their lips, but she never knew. He said to her, "Now don't you go and throw something at them, ma'am, it would not be proper in someone in your position and you might never know what you got back." "Go away," she said out loud again.

Although all those windows had been shut there was a continual dull roar came through them from outside, and this noise sat upon those within like clouds upon a mountain so they were obscured and levelled and, as though they had been airmen, in danger of running fatally into earth. Clouds also, if they are banked up, will so occupy the sky as to dwarf what is beneath and this low roar, which was only conversation in that multitude without, lay over them in such a pall, like night coming on and there is no light when one must see, that these people here were obscured by it and were dimmed into anxious Roman numerals.

Not putting this into words he did feel relieved when he got into a passage where it was emptier, though three people lay at full length against one wall. Seeing another stranger come out of one door to go into another, "Hi, Charlie," he shouted, not knowing his name, and stopped him. These three sleepers moaned in their darkness. "Charlie," he went on, coming up to him, "any way out of 'ere?" "No, lad, it's all shut up." "But say you or me wanted to get out?" "He'd slip out of a window," this other stranger said and went off.

"Have you looked outside?" Julia said to Evelyn upstairs.

"How d'you mean, outside?"

"Why at all those millions down below," she said, and led them past where Angela was sitting by the curtains. "Look at that, darlings," she said almost tearfully, for what had exhilarated her not so long ago was forbidding now. She frowned.

Max came back to be with them, unseeing. Now that he had heard Amabel and that he knew she was in her bath undressed, it seemed to him that when they had been together she had warmed him every side. When he opened his eyes close beside her in the flat she had blotted out the light, only where her eye would be he could see dazzle, all the rest of her mountain face had been that dark acreage against him. He had lain in the shadow of it under softly beaten wings of her breathing, and his thoughts, hatching up out of sleep, had bundled back into the other darkness of her plumes. So being entirely delivered over he had lain still, he remembered, because he had been told by that dazzle her eyelids were not down so that she lay still awake.

He wanted her.

So this stranger on his mission went into rooms at a venture, tried windows and found them locked, and then went out again until he came to one room where two maids leant out of an open casement towards their knight standing on his friend's shoulder from the station floor ten foot beneath. His bowler hat lay next his friend's feet and in a cross neatly on the crown of it lay his pair of gloves.

Through this open window noise of all those outside smote him in one vast confused hum like numbers of aeroplanes flying by and against which these two maids' shrill female voices, screeching to make themselves appreciated by their white-collared boy, were like urgent wheels that had not been oiled. Interfering again he came forward and he said, "Save us, young fellow. Don't you go and fall down or you might be hurt."

"It's her eyes enfold me and uphold me," was his gallant answer.

"Did you hear that?" she screeched, and her friend leaned further out and said:

"Which one, which eyes?"

"Now don't make me choose," he said, reaching up with one arm, his other hand sucking to the wall. "Hold me," he said, "hold me." One of them stretched her dainty dirty fingers down and he caught her wrist. "Now," he said, "where would you be if I jumped off his shoulder?" These two screamed now like rats smelling food when they have been starved in empty milk-churns. "Listen," this stranger interrupted, "that's murder," leaning out himself. "What's murder?" was his answer, and the other said he could not stand Ed's weight much longer. They redoubled their shrieks, they were famished and had not been so charmed for ages.

"She'd fall slap on her 'ead and break 'er neck," he said pondering, when the one who was being held broke off her shrieks to say, well it was her neck, wasn't it?

"I'll jump off and then I'll knock his block off for him," he murmured and scrambled out, hung at arm's length, while Ed said, mind my gloves and hat, dropped lightly for his age, and began ploughing his way through. He had forgotten them at once.

To push through this crowd was like trying to get through bamboo or artichokes grown thick together or thousands of tailors' dummies stored warm on a warehouse floor.

"What targets," one by him remarked, "what targets for a bomb."

Max leaned his forehead against a shut window tormented by his dreams of Amabel, daydreams brought on by her voice, by her being so near, by her choosing to be undressed behind that door and because she used another voice when she wore no clothes, she mocked.

He was in that state when she no longer haunted him all day, but it came back at night and when, if thinking about her while she was not there did not make him as desperate as he had once been when first he knew her he still had that same feeling come over him at times and all the more, very often, when they had just met again.

Five months ago, when his love had been first conceived, he had been maddened by his thoughts of her when she was away, they had boiled all over him and then when she came back they would simmer down again to his happiness. But now he was cooling off he still had returns of that old feeling made worse because he resented her still having that command.

She still swayed him like water moves a trailing weed, and froth and some little dirt collects round, and sometimes when he first heard her voice again and when as now she used that private tone, then it was as if his tide had turned and helpless he was turned back, delivered up to move to her tune and trail back the way he had come helpless, delivered over, benighted.

And as does, in moonlight in cold deep-shadowed other day, push him out of his burrow and kick the old buck to death so when they saw him down, these girls and Amabel, coming out as she now did, all set upon him he was so absurd.

"Look round, darling," Amabel said as cruel as could be, "I'm here, not floating around outside." Angel, he said to himself, angel and knew how fatuous it was and could not help himself. When he did turn round to say how do you do, like Robin Adams he could not bring himself to look at her and this made him seem ashamed.

"Hamlet," said Julia, and then all three girls laughed.

"Well, my darlings, and what shall we do?" she went on and laughed twice, for Max had turned his back again, he looked so like any boy at school, "here we are, three lovely girls all mewed up and can't get out. What d'you say?"

Amabel smiled at his back as though she was taken up with thinking all of him over. She held a bone paper knife against her cheek, along her nose now and then across her forehead. She thought these three bits prettiest in her face.

Angela said how lovely her dressing gown and bent down to stroke it and Amabel murmured Embassy Richard had given it her. So all three of them laughed again, and Amabel said, "I'm so bored, darling." They were in league against him and watched his back like cats over offal or as if they thought his heart might fall out at their feet feebly smiling and stuck all over with darts or safety pins.

Miss Crevy asked where Alex had got to and Julia said, why didn't she know he was up to his old tricks with Toddy, how he adored her, for as soon as Amabel looked another way he would always be after her maid.

"Is she so very pretty then?"

Julia laughed and explained she was ever so old and besides hadn't Angela seen her in here already and Amabel sat on, quite still and quiet, looking at his back.

"Lot of people down there," he said at last.

Julia thought she would take him in hand. "Max, why don't you turn round and entertain us?" she said and smiled at Amabel who smiled back. "You do look such a silly standing there as if they'd made you dunce or put you in coventry or something."

But this shot went too near home. Amabel said again and this time more kindly, "I'm so bored, darling," for she did not care to let them go too far with him.

He turned round and again could not bring himself to raise his eyes. He said:

"There's nothing for it," and at that he saw her feet which were bare in sandals and looked fantastic on that cheap carpet. Her toes were pink and quite perfect for him, so much so they had no character at all and he thought they were unreal. The nails glittered.

"Are you going to go out like that?" he said.

"I might."

He still looked at her toes and while she watched his face she began to move them one after another. He quickly dared one look at her face to see what she was driving at and what he saw, remembered beauty, turned his heart to stone so tight that he smiled into her jewelled eyes like any Fido asking for his bone. Now she was back he was delivered up for punishment, only wanting to be slaves again. She looked hard at him. "Oh, God," he said and turned away again.

Julia laughed. "Max," she said, "we're here, this way, and not out there. Oh, d'you remember," she went on, "that time we were out at Svengalo's when the mad waiter, that one who never finished rearranging one's knives and forks, began to lose his trousers, they simply began to slip down like petticoats and he never knew? It was Embassy Richard had unbuttoned him and he had no idea, d'you all remember how Max got up and went out on us, because he couldn't take it, and there we were left to blush?"

"Oh, no!" said Angela, who had not been with them.

"Amabel, d'you remember it?" Julia went on, "and then we never saw that mad waiter again, Svengalo sacked him for not minding his trousers, so they all use safety pins now, the other waiters. Richard said Svengalo does too, he'd tried the other night. Come back to us, Max darling."

As he made no reply she went on:

"And do you remember that time I fainted and you took me outside and that drunk made a pass at me when you had stretched me out? Shall I ever let you forget how you left me at once after I was better and went right away? And didn't come back. Defenceless, mind you, or almost, against that gorilla and he was so beastly drunk he didn't know what he was doing except when he picked on me. Why do you go away, Max?"

"Yes," Amabel said, "why do you leave us?" and all he could find to say was well he was here, wasn't he, speaking with his back still turned to them.

"But then what on earth happened to you?" Angela said.

"Oh, well, you see there were others in our party, there always are," Julia said and she looked at Angela gravely, "but wasn't it beastly of him, Am?" she said, turning to her, but Amabel was looking at her toes. "And then there was that time when he walked out on you, Am, and I said you can't do that, go back. D'you remember? It was that night we went out by car to bathe and the farmer thought we had no clothes on. And when life's so short."

"Did you say that then, darling?" Amabel said and smiled sweetly up at her.

"But what are you thinking of, darling, it was Mr. Hignam, no less, said it to Claire of course, though what he can have meant I can't imagine." She smiled as sweetly back.

"When was this, do tell me?" Angela said.

"Not for your ears, darling," and while she said this Amabel kept her eyes on Julia. She began to move her toes again.

"But why, my dear, what's this?" said Julia, because nothing had happened then or she would have remembered. But she saw how Amabel did not know this, or did not mean to see it.

"Well, really," Julia said, "well, well."

Max had turned round. He looked at each in turn.

"Hey," he said, "what's this?"

"That night when we went to bathe," said Amabel.

"Which one?"

"When the farmer thought Julia had no clothes on."

"Yes."

"And you wondered too."

"I wondered?"

"Oh no, he didn't," Julia said and laughed quite differently.

"By God Max," Amabel said, "the way you go on with my friends," she said, although Max had first introduced Julia to her and they had never become friends.

"No, darling, really, I had on my flesh-coloured suit."

"I don't remember anything."

"Well, if you don't remember," Amabel said to him, "I should think you were tight. Anyway, by the way you went on in my car afterwards you would be."

"You think I have to get tight to..." he said and broke off and this made Amabel laugh. It seemed to her she had sufficiently established her claim over him, so she laughed again.

And Julia laughed to save her face and lastly Angela laughed to keep in with them.

"Oh, you know what I mean," he said.

"We know," Miss Crevy said.

"Oh, do you, darling?" said Amabel and getting up she stepped forward and kissed him and then stayed by, leaving her face close to his. He found her hair was still damp and this tortured him for something he remembered of her once and then it came over him she meant to put him through it before the others. And then because he had realized this it put him right, he felt he had seen through her little game and anyway he thought with glee what were they doing but fighting over him so that he grinned with confidence right into her mouth. She gave way at once, half opened her jaws and sat down again. He could see her pink tongue. She looked tired and older. He laughed.

"You think I have..." he said and laughed once more.

"Why not?" said Julia and turned away, thinking this was disgusting.

"Why not what?" he said.

"Oh, get tight or anything."

"Who said anything about getting tight?" for he had already forgotten anyone had spoken about getting drunk he felt so relieved. As if he had escaped, as indeed he had back into slavery again or as if his punishment was over, while it was just preparing. And now Julia was caught back into her old misery, so much so she felt she could not bear it and must get out of here so she went outside to find Claire and Evelyn.

"Why don't you tell me about all these thrilling parties and things? What happened with Farmer Bangs?" Miss Crevy said.

"Oh, nothing."

"No, Max, it was obviously something thrilling."

"We went out to bathe."

"Well?"

"And Am said we ought to go back."

"Well?" she said and got no reply; he was looking at Amabel.

"Yes?" she said.

"You know how it is."

"That's just what I don't know."

He was the one who laughed now. He laughed and said:

"Then you'd better learn."

"Not knowing isn't the same as not having learned."

"What is it then?"

"Isn't he extraordinary?" she said to Amabel, but got no help from her, she was looking at her toes. "My dear Max," she went on, "even if I do know all the answers it doesn't mean I know what went on that evening."

"You can guess then."

This was rude but she was not going to give in to any of them again, not even to Max.

"But what did the farmer say?" she said and had no answer.

"Oh, come on," she said and stamped her foot.

"Oh, what did he say?" she said again.

"Darling," said Amabel turning to her, "he said them that are asked no questions won't be told no lies." Max laughed and said it wasn't him so much, it was his dog. And at this, although she had not been gone more than three minutes, Julia came back to them. "My dear," she said to Max, ignoring those others, "I'm afraid Claire's Auntie May is rather bad."

"Rather bad you say?" he repeated after her, not having taken this in.

"Yes, rather bad I said, though I think it's worse than that."

"I can't help it," he said. "She's got a room, hasn't she?" and Amabel asked him if Claire's aunt was coming on their party too, and he laughed and said he did not know.

"How can you stand there and laugh, Max darling, really," Julia said, not because she was worried about how ill the old thing might be but so as to get him out of this room, no matter how.

"I say," he said, rising, "that's bad."

"I thought you ought to know."

He stood quiet. Amabel was looking at Julia. "Poor Claire," she said, "what a shame."

"What about a doctor?"

"Oh, they had one in hours ago, Max."

"What did he say?" Angela said, getting finally in on this story at last. And Julia, realizing, felt she ought to explain, and while she was explaining thought she would pass over what the doctor really said about Miss Fellowes, they would only laugh when they heard and Max would pay no more attention. "Well, you see, Angela darling, Claire did not want anyone to know, you know how people are that way. Anyway," she said, lying, "I believe this aunt of hers asked Claire not to say one word to anyone; you see she felt she had been trouble enough already, Max had been perfectly sweet and taken her a room. She did not want to be any more bother, did she, because after all we are supposed to be going off on our holiday, aren't we? But still, Max, my dear, there it is and I thought you ought to know. As a matter of fact the doctor was very worried about her."

"What did he do?" said Max.

"What did he do?" she echoed, "why, what do doctors do? Of course he got his fee, Robert paid him, but you know what they are; he went away again; she might die for all he cared."

"Where is Robert?" he said. He could not bear it if anyone in any party of his paid for anything.

"Downstairs in the bar. Why?" she said.

"Can't have that, you know."

"Oh, Max, you are sweet!" she said, "but really, after all, it is his own aunt and she was not in our party; really she's got nothing to do with you."

Amabel asked herself why then come to bother him about this old trout, and then told herself she knew.

"Can't have it," he said cheerfully, as people do when they are living up to their own characters.

"Darling," said Amabel, "don't be so like yourself."

"I wish you would help," Julia said and then thought why not put it on to Claire. "Poor Claire," she went on, "she is so worried."

"What's that crack for?" he said to Amabel.

"What crack?"

"Don't be so like yourself or something?"

"Oh, nothing," she said and smiled up at him as if he enormously amused her.

"Well, if that's all," he said still looking at her, "then I'd better go see what can be done."

"But I mean," said Angela, and they all turned surprised for they had forgotten her, "I mean would Claire like that? I thought she wanted nobody to know," she said with malice.

"Claire's upset, poor darling, it's horrible for her," Julia explained and at this moment Alex came back in again.

"There's no one anywhere like your Toddy," he said to Amabel and looked tremendously pleased. "The things I've found out about you, you'll never be able to be quite the same to me again with all I've got on you now. Really Am, it's fantastic, you can't imagine, I mean it makes coming and all this waiting worth while. Not of course that it isn't heaven our all being here together and all that, only there is so little to do, but have baths and gossip. Why, what's the matter, it's nothing I've said or done is it? You all look as if you'd been at one of my uncle Joe's board meetings."

"It's about Claire's aunt, this Miss Fellowes. She's very ill."

"I know all about it, Julia, you told me ages ago and tried to be frightfully mysterious about it."

"I'm very worried about her."

"I'll bet you aren't really," he said, "and if she's going to die, even, what difference—"

"Oh, no, Alex," she said.

"—does it make to you?" he went on, and she said "Alex, no, no," again. "Well," he said, "we've all got to come to it some time, though why it should be here of all places I can't imagine." While he was talking Miss Crevy looked at him with loathing. "Oh, I know," he went on, "I know she's not so bad as all that but I don't care anyhow and I advise everyone to feel the same. Otherwise I shall go home," he said, blushing with anger all of a sudden, "yes, and I shall advise everyone to do the same. We all fuss too much."

"Really, Alex," said Julia and was staggered, "what has come over you? I don't think you are being very polite, are you?"

"When is he ever?" said Miss Crevy.

"Yes," he said, quickly recovering himself, "like the cornet player said at the Salvation Army meeting, 'I'll give you one more 'oly 'oly 'oly and then I'm off 'ome.'"

They did not know what to make of this so Max said "Good for you, Alex," and Amabel said to him, "Darling, tell me something very nice." At this Alex smiled, sat on the arm of her chair and turned round to look into her face. She smiled sideways at him and as always when she smiled so far as he was concerned it was so brilliant it made him shy. She then reached out and with one long vermilion finger-nail she began to scratch gently at one of his knuckles, for she liked making him shy, he who was not supposed to care about girls. He thought how much cleaner her wrist was than his hand it lay across and how much stronger it looked than you would expect, but then of course she was probably extremely powerful and he always had thought women were more powerful than men. And so, as she scratched gently she began to gain power over him and he felt himself slipping away she did it so well, just right, so that if he had been her pussy cat he would have purred. He was going to shut down his eyes and give himself over to sleep, it was stretching up over him from his hand when he lazily thought he must look ridiculous and this at once went through him as if he was being rung up so that he hung up on her, drawing away out of reach. For two minutes she went on gently scratching at the chair arm. It was embarrassment on his part, he was afraid he would be made to look foolish and she knew this very well. She went on smiling at him without any change of expression and still sideways, almost as though what she had begun with him she had put over on herself as well.

The others went on talking, Max was quite forthcoming now, and as no one paid them any attention he thought what a pity, and this was what she meant him to feel, why if he was left on a desert island with this girl he would only count what nuts there might be on those spreading awkward palms for fear monkeys should see him. Not looking at her he put his hand out again and having won she laughed and only patted it once and then turned to those others again. He laughed and said:

"I missed my chance."

She turned back to him for an instant and he saw from her eyes she was not bothering any more about him. When she did not smile her eyes were not so blue but now she smiled, patted him once again, and finally left him though he had only to stretch out to take hold of her dressing-gown and she was wearing nothing underneath.

"I always do," he said, but she did not come back so he tried one last time, "miss my chance," he said, but it was no good and he gave up trying. He did not see that she had kept him with them, not knowing whether he really meant to go home. Her purpose was to keep them round her to show herself off in front of Max.

"No," Max was saying, "particularly now that Claire has her aunt down with something I don't see how we can go home. No need for you others to stay, of course; and for the matter of that there's nothing to be done about her, is there? But I ought to stay."

"But, Max," said Julia, "as Evelyn said while we were outside, it's all very well talking of going home, but they won't keep the train waiting when they do send it off just for us to come and catch it. If anyone goes they'll miss it."

"I'm sorry, everybody, it was my idea about waiting at home," Alex said, "but I was in a filthy mood. I didn't mean it."

"What I mean is," said Max, "I could have you rung up if you all went back to my flat. They would let me know when they were going to send our train off in time to get you here." And as he said this he was well aware that Julia's uncle was a director of this line but he liked better to make out they would do all this for him. However, Julia agreed with Evelyn, and felt so strongly about it she almost made a scene. She said if they once left they would never get back again and she described how much thicker it was the way she had come than it really had been and made so much fuss they had to give in largely out of a loyalty all felt to her moods, all that is except Miss Crevy. When she had had her way she said why didn't they get Claire and Evelyn to leave Miss Fellowes and come along to join them, surely they could risk that, she could not be so bad those old nannies could not see to her. Max approved of this and went to fetch them.

"Will anyone have a drink?" said Alex, "I fancy it would do us all some good," but no one answered and now that Max was no longer with them Angela and Julia had nothing to say, nor had Amabel. He wondered how often this had happened to him before and marvelled again that anyone should be so run after as Max, though never so run after in such an awful room before. Places alter circumstances, he thought, and there was little amusing in being ignored in these surroundings, armchairs that were too deep with too narrow backs and covered in modified plush, that is plush with the pile shaved off so that those chairs were to him like so many clean-shaven port drinkers.

Clean-shaven port drinkers enough, he went on, mixing his drink, one for each girl, that is three chairs but only Amabel sitting on those gouty knees, that sodden lap; and then public house lace curtains to guard them in from fog and how many naked bodies on sentry go underneath adequately, inadequately dressed. Here he pointed his moral. That is what it is to be rich, he thought, if you are held up, if you have to wait then you can do it after a bath in your dressing-gown and if you have to die then not as any bird tumbling dead from its branch down for the foxes, light and stiff, but here in bed, here inside, with doctors to tell you it is all right and with relations to ask if it hurts. Again no standing, no being pressed together, no worry since it did not matter if one went or stayed, no fellow feeling, true, and once more sounds came up from outside to make him think they were singing, no community singing he said to himself, not that even if it did mean fellow feeling. And in this room, as always, it seemed to him there was a sort of bond between the sexes and with these people no more than that, only dull antagonism otherwise. But not in this room he said to himself again, not with that awful central light, that desk at which no one had ever done more than pay bills or write their dentist, no, no, not here, not thus. Never again, he swore, but not aloud, never again in this world because it was too boring and he had done it so many times before.

It was all the fault of these girls. It had been such fun in old days when they had just gone and no one had minded what happened. They had been there to enjoy themselves and they had been friends but if you were girls and went on a party then it seemed to him you thought only of how you were doing, of how much it looked to others you were enjoying yourself and worse than that of how much whoever might be with you could give you reasons for enjoying it. Or, in other words, you competed with each other in how well you were doing well and doing well was getting off with the rich man in the party. Whoever he might be such treatment was bad for him. Max was not what he had been. No one could have people fighting over him and stay himself. It was not Amabel's fault, she was all right even if she did use him, it was these desperate inexperienced bitches, he thought, who never banded together but fought everyone and themselves and were like camels, they could go on for days without one sup of encouragement. Under their humps they had tanks of self-confidence so that they could cross any desert area of arid prickly pear without one compliment, or dewdrop as they called it in his family, to uphold them. So bad for the desert, he said to himself, developing his argument and this made him laugh aloud.

"What are you laughing about?" said Julia, who felt out of whatever Max was doing with himself outside.

"Oh, nothing," he said.

"I do hate people who go away, darling," she said to Amabel, "not physically I mean," she said, catching herself up, "but when they are in a room and then they go and leave one." But while Amabel had been ready to take this up where Max was concerned, Alex did not exist for her any more and her answer was to send him for her nail things with another smile just as brilliantly blue as when she had been thinking of him. And now, when for the moment he was gone, silence fell over them with lifeless wings.

While he was away, which was not for long, no one spoke. Amabel looked at her nails from which she was going to take one coloured varnish to put on another. Julia fidgeted with the cuff of what she was wearing and Miss Crevy examined her face in a mirror out of her bag like any jeweller with a precious stone, and it was indeed without price, but it had its ticket and this had Marriage written on it.

When he came back and gave Amabel what she wanted he was struck again by how glum they seemed. He said into their silence, "and to think this is supposed to be the happiest time of our lives." Julia did not understand. "Why now exactly?" she said from far away. "Well, we're young," he said, "we'll never be young again you see." "Why aren't you happy then?" she said, as though she was on an ivory tower. "That's not the point," said he, his eyes on Amabel, "but I'm so bored." "Aren't we all?" she said and because she thought this sort of conversation silly Miss Crevy broke in by asking Amabel what kind of nail polish she used. Already the acetone she had filled this room with its smell of peardrops like a terrible desert blossom. He coughed, it stifled him.

"I was wondering if I wouldn't make them darker," she said, "like the sloe gin Max gives me out shooting."

"What's that?" said Angela.

"It's more like port, isn't it?" Julia said to show she had been out with him too. "Oh, do you remember?" she asked, though as she did it now it was almost automatic as though it was her part she had to play to evoke good times, alone, on top of this ivory tower with his dreaming world beneath, sleeping beauty, all of them folded so she imagined into their thoughts of him. "Amabel," she said, "d'you remember that time it was corked?" But she said it so low, so quietly this time that no one followed her. Memory is a winding lane and as she went up it, waving them to follow, the first bend in it hid her from them and she was left to pick her flowers alone.

Memory is a winding lane with high banks on which flowers grow and here she wandered in a nostalgic summer evening in deep soundlessness.

Angela went back to her mirror and began touching the tips of her eyelashes with her fingers' ends. Alex picked up a newspaper and behind it picked his nose.

Night was coming up and it came out of the sea. Over harbours, up the river, by factories, bringing lights in windows and lamps on the streets until it met this fog where it lay and poured more darkness in.

Fog burdened with night began to roll into this station striking cold through thin leather up into their feet where in thousands they stood and waited. Coils of it reached down like women's long hair reached down and caught their throats and veiled here and there what they could see, like lovers' glances. A hundred cold suns switched on above found out these coils where, before the night joined in, they had been smudges and looking up at two of them above was like she was looking down at you from under long strands hanging down from her forehead only that light was cold and these curls tore at your lungs.

It was not comfortable and there were signs that this long wait was beginning to fray tempers. At first there had been patient jokes and then some community singing but nice as these had been and as everyone had felt in taking all this nicely, it was beginning to wear thin until only those who were getting off with girls could say they were enjoying themselves. They searched round and about picking and choosing. "I hope you don't mind my speaking to you," they would say or "I don't know when we shall get back, do you?" or "I say this is very unconventional my speaking to you like this," although they had wifey and the couple of kids at home. These girls, and many of them had been chosen for their looks where they worked, were so sick and tired, and this kind of approach was so much more reason for tiredness, they turned away with no words to answer them, disgusted.

There was nothing wonderful or strange in what they saw. For any of these people, night ended once a night and was only remembered by some of them for a person the moon that certain night had shone on in their arms, those loving arms. And when fog was joined to night who was there to dream of that cruel oblivion of sight it made when they had in mind chintz curtains waiting to be drawn across shut windows.

Again, being in it, how was it possible for them to view themselves as part of that vast assembly for even when they had tried singing they had only heard those next them; it was impossible to tell if all had joined except when, perhaps at the end of a verse, one section made themselves heard as they were late and had not yet finished. Then everyone knew everyone was singing but this feeling did not last and soon they did not agree about songs, that section would be going on while another sang one of their own. Then no one sang at all.

So crowded together they were beginning to be pressed against each other, so close that every breath had been inside another past that lipstick or those cracked lips, those even teeth, loose dentures, down into other lungs, so weary, so desolate and cold it silenced them.

Then one section had begun to chant "we want our train" over and over again and at first everyone had laughed and joined in and then had failed, there were no trains. And so, having tried everything, desolation overtook them.

They were like ruins in the wet, places that is where life has been, palaces, abbeys, cathedrals, throne rooms, pantries, cast aside and tumbled down with no immediate life and with what used to be in them lost rather than hidden now the roof has fallen in. Ruins that is not of their suburban homes for they had hearts, and feelings to dream, and hearts to make up what they did not like into other things. But ruins, for life in such circumstances was only possible because it would not last, only endurable because it had broken down and as it lasted and became more desolate and wet so, as it seemed more likely to be permanent, at least for an evening, they grew restive.

Where ruins lie, masses of stone grown over with ivy unidentifiable with the mortar fallen away so that stone lies on stone loose and propped up or crumbling down in mass then as a wind starts up at dusk and stirs the ivy leaves and rain follows slanting down, so deserted no living thing seeks what little shelter there may be, it is all brought so low, then movements of impatience began to flow across all these people and as ivy leaves turn one way in the wind they themselves surged a little here and there in their blind search behind bowler hats and hats for trains.

But at one point no movement showed where, like any churchyard, gravestone luggage waited with mourners, its servants and owners, squatted in between. Here Thomson, still without his tea, had not forgotten yet that kiss she had blessed him with and went rambling on, both aloud and in his mind, how he could not bear that she had been called away. Every now and again he would get up to look over the monuments about, but she was no longer with those other mourners who glared back at him for intruding on their lives in the little rooms their luggage made them. Indeed one old lady had gone so far as to get her "Primus" out and was making tea as though playing at Indians in second childhood and Thomson was telling Edwards he was sure this was his girl's party and how if that old creature had not been there he might have had his tea and kisses too. Edwards asked him to beware, saying so much imagination must be bad for anyone, let alone somebody as crazy as he seemed to be.

"Only crazy for what I haven't got," he said, "like any drowning, starving man."

"Drowning are you now? I'd have sworn you was like any little schoolboy with his first sweetheart, his pretty honeypot."

"All right, but it's natural, isn't it, same as it is to want a cup of tea." He went on that if someone were to come now and offer him half a dollar for this luggage he would accept if it did mean his job, or he would for a cup of tea even. Edwards said now he was back harping on it, "your jew's harp," he went on, straining his fancy, "always wanting more than what you have."

But Thomson's trouble was sex. He could not hold that kiss she had given him as it might be an apple in his hand to turn over while he made up his mind to bite, he was like any starving creature who wanted one more apple and this made him restless. And this was why, though he did not know it, he went on about his tea. He always had a cup of tea if his mind ran for too long on girls, that is when he had no girl ready to his hand.

"It's not my tea so much," he said, expressing this.

"You want the moon," said Edwards.

Meantime Robert Hignam's man, who had so frightened Julia, was making his way from one grieving mourner to another or, as they sat abandoned, cast away each by his headstone, they were like the dead resurrected in their clothes under this cold veiled light and in an antiseptic air. He dodged about asking any man he saw if he was Miss Julia Wray's, so much as to say, "I be the grave-digger, would I bury you again?"

When he found Thomson he tried to persuade him to hand the luggage over so that he could get it into the hotel because he wanted to be clever and do more than Robert had required. Thomson asked who had sent him and when he heard it was Hignam he said he could not take orders from any but Miss Wray. Edwards said who was he anyway, he might be Arsene Lupin easy, and what did he take them for?

"Well, as you might say, the orders did come from that young lady."

"Tell us," said Thomson and Edwards could not understand how he could go on talking with this man who might be anybody, "what's going on in there?" he said, nodding over to where they were sitting quarrelling up above behind lace curtains.

"She's a goner."

"Who's a goner?"

"Why that young lady's aunt."

"Don't talk so silly," Edwards said.

"As sure as I'm here," he answered.

"Have you seen her?"

"Of course I've seen her," he said, speaking in educated tones again. "She was taken bad in the buffet and they had to carry her upstairs."

"And what about a doctor?"

"Ah," he said, "they've had the doctor to her, but he's no doctor, I've not been around all these years without I know about that hotel doctor. He's killed any number of them," he said, "when they've been carried in," and as he talked of death his speech relapsed into some dialect of his own, "any bloody number of 'em," he went on, "as've been took bad on the bloody Continent and 'ave said well if they were going to be sick they'd be sick in their own native land and so left it too late, appendicitis and all," he said.

"Not bloody likely," said Edwards, any talk of death making him swear.

"It's the bloody truth."

"Well then," said Edwards, "if anything was to come to her, it's unpack for you and me, my lad," he said to Thomson.

At this a huge wild roar broke from the crowd. They were beginning to adjust that board indicating times of trains which had stood all of two hours behind where it had reached when first the fog came down.

"Wild animals," Edwards said.

"Won't do her any good," said Hignam's man.

"Well, that's a shocking thing," Thomson said, "if anything were to happen to Miss Fellowes, why my young lady wouldn't half take on, you know, soft 'earted."

"Death's a bloody awful thing," said Edwards, "but it isn't as easy as all that, it takes time to die. She couldn't have been well enough to come all that way here if she was going to die this minute. Depend upon it she's all right, or will be."

"Well," said Thomson, "I reckon if what he says is right it will put paid to this party, they'll all be off 'ome and we'll get no thanks for it."

Edwards remarked Miss Fellowes had been acting very extraordinary before, very extraordinary, but that did not mean anything except she had come over queer.

"And shall I take these things?" this strange man said.

"Where's a copper?"

"Who are you talking to, young feller?"

"Go on and get off," said Edwards, "we've had enough of you and now you've bloody well upset me with your talk. Who'd you think is going to give you his luggage, now get on, go off."

He went and Thomson said some people did have strange ideas. Now who would imagine he would try to go through all that mob with valuable luggage, just so as Miss Julia could see it was still there, when she hadn't even said she wanted to. But it did seem this man knew something about them and it was rotten about Miss Fellowes. If she was ill why they'd none of them start, they'd put it off as sure as anything.

Edwards said not to be too sure, she was no relation of theirs, meaning Mr. Adey's and Miss Wray's. He'd known worse happen without his gentleman turning back.

"Well, it wouldn't be right, not to start like that, not with that behind you," said Thomson. "And if she did die why you'd never be the same, none of them would, not for three days at all events."

"And I thought you wanted your tea so bad you'd have given all this away for sixpence."

"Oh, that was different," said Thomson, meaning his Emily.

"But then would you go, you," he went on, "if anything of that kind was to happen?"

"No, I would not," said Edwards, "but then they're different."

"It's all the old same, excuse me," Thomson said, "death's death, if you understand me."

"Let's get this straight. No one except that loony said she was going to die, did they?"

"Well, it's the same if she was really bad, they'd never go."

"Mr. Adey would."

"And my young lady wouldn't."

"Don't you be so sure, my lad. I fancy she'd follow him all over, or she'd like to."

"I won't speak about that if you don't mind," said Thomson, "I don't hold with following what anyone's after or saying this or that about them. What they do is none of my concern. No, I don't like it," he said and probably did not know what he really meant. Anyway they both of them dropped it.

But this was what Claire was talking about with Evelyn. Max was in her bedroom with those two old nannies and they were standing in the corridor outside.

"What do you think?" Claire said to her.

"I know," said Evelyn, "it's very worrying isn't it?"

"What would you do?"

"I don't know."

"You see what so upsets me is when one of them in there says, and I don't know which of the old things it was, mine or the other, did you hear it, she said 'oh no, dearie, why you couldn't go now, not with your own aunt lying there.' When she calls me dearie it makes me feel like a street woman. And that when the doctor said it was nothing, or anyway if it wasn't nothing that it wasn't serious. Evelyn, my dear, when anyone is as drunk as that they sleep it off, don't they, I mean they don't lie there unconscious and after all she has passed out now hasn't she, that is she lies there breathing in that awful way she's not asleep is she? I don't know, if we could get hold of another doctor he might be able to tell us something, but then I don't want to seem nasty and I hate to say it but supposing he said she was very bad, well then, it would not help her if we went or stayed, would it? Oh, can you tell me why that idiot Robert doesn't do something?"

Evelyn did not reply. Claire seemed to ponder for a moment. "D'you think it would do any good if we tried to make her sick again?"

"Oh, no, I shouldn't."

"Well, after all, that's what the doctor said was the matter, didn't he? But then it's so impossible, Evelyn darling, why I've known Auntie May all my life, she couldn't be like this because of that. And I couldn't tell my own nanny about what the doctor said about mother's sister, could I? You do agree, don't you?"

"Of course."

"But then you see I can't help feeling they may be right. After all, what could that doctor know about poor Auntie May, he may have just said to himself here's another old lady who likes port too much. And we can't get her out of here, and any minute just because Julia's uncle or guardian is a director of the railway they may come and tell us we must go. D'you think I ought to stay behind and perhaps come on afterwards?"

"Well, she lives alone, doesn't she, I mean she hasn't got anybody."

"Those nannies could look after her, they've got absolutely nothing to do, you know, they are pensioned off, mine just lives at home, at number nine I mean and drinks tea all day. Besides she nursed me through several very serious illnesses and with all that experience and being so fond of the family she would be better than any trained nurse, they never care whether you live or die."

"You mean there's no one else to look after her."

"No, there's absolutely no one. There's her maid and I don't know why we didn't make her come round when it first started, you remember I rang her up telling her to stay away. I can't imagine why but of course she has fits, no, absolutely everyone else is dead and mother's abroad as you know. It's rather touching, that's why she came to see us off really, it's her only link. No, but it's not touching actually because she goes and gets ill. Oh, Evelyn, it's so unfair, isn't it?"

And as she said this surprisingly she began to cry, not sobbing or that free flow out of a contorted face, but it was as though some miracle had occurred, as though tears were gently one by one rolling down graven image features which had stayed dry under cover for centuries, carved out of hard wood, so that these tears threatened to crack a polished surface it looked so unused to being wetted, only creamed.

"Oh, my dear," said Evelyn, "you mustn't let yourself get upset about this business and besides I think you've been perfectly wonderful about it all the way through, you've hardly left her for an instant."

"It's not that," she said, and she spoke as though she were not crying, her tears seemed to be quite separate from her, only a phenomenon, "it's that I feel the whole thing is so unfair. I do know Julia is rather counting on having me with her this trip and now that Amabel has dropped out of the sky I do deeply feel I can't let her down." This was untrue. She went on and as people will when they have just lied she began to speak out genuinely for once what she did really feel. "What I'm so afraid of is that doctor had no idea what he was talking about, that Aunt May is very bad and that I ought to get her to hospital and I am doing nothing about it. I ought not to be here," she said, "but you know how it is, I thought it was just a faint and that she would come round and that after a bit of rest she would be able to go home. One thing you can be quite sure of is that she's not drunk, poor darling, she probably felt it coming over her whatever it is and took something to keep it off." Her tears had stopped now. "But then you see," she went on, "there's no way of getting her out of here though if she was really bad of course the hotel would manage it somehow you know how they are."

"Don't."

"Well, there's no blinking it you know, they would if they thought she was going to die."

"Then oughtn't we to send for her maid whatever her name is?"

"Yes, if she could get in. And then she has fits."

"Good heavens, we don't want two on our hands."

"She probably had one when I rang up an hour ago. I don't know what to do," she said. "Sorry for crying," and she began to powder her nose.

"I think what we are both afraid of," said Evelyn, "is that parcel she had and what was inside it. She never belonged to any societies for animals, did she? She never kept pigeons herself I mean?"

"Of course not. Besides she used to shoot."

"You know I have absolute faith in searching out whatever it is that is really worrying one underneath what seems on the surface to be the matter with anything if you understand me, Claire, my dear. And I know in my case it was her having picked that pigeon up somewhere and then seeming so ill. She can't have bought it or she would have had it delivered, unless she got it off a barrow, but then they don't sell them on barrows. D'you see what I mean? But if she just found it dead and picked it up what did she want it for, it was so dirty? I'm sure that's what's been worrying us, but when you come to think of it, darling, there's nothing in it, is there? What is it after all? Now if it had been a goose or some other bird. No, that isn't so I don't suppose it would have been any less odd. Anyway it is definitely not a thing to worry about."

At this moment Max came out of her room.

"She's better," he said.

"Max, dear," said Claire, "you've been too sweet about it all, getting her this lovely room and everything, I don't know how to thank you, it's been too kind of you."

"Nonsense," he said, "bad business. Where's Robert?"

"Oh, my dear," she said, "don't ask me that. Where do you suppose, in the Bar I should think." At this Amabel appeared in a fur coat and drew him away, and as Claire hurried back in with Evelyn she said to herself how like a man to come out as if he had settled everything and made her better just by going in.

She was better, but they could not help feeling that she was improving only to get worse. She lay fretful and conscious, propped up in bed.

"Why am I here?" she said.

"Oh, Auntie May, you are ever so much better, aren't you? Now you mustn't lie there worrying, just relax?"

"Where am I?"

"Now don't bother your head about anything, you're quite all right and now you are going to have a nice long rest."

"What happened to me?"

"You mustn't bother your head about anything like that. Nothing happened to you really, you just fainted. Now lie back and get back your strength."

"Excuse me," she said, and her one eye you could see looked agitated, "no, child I never fainted, I never have."

"Oh, Auntie May, how could you be so naughty, you'll upset yourself in a minute, do be careful after all. You've made us all quite anxious, well not that exactly," she said, because those two old nannies had shaken their heads at this, "but, of course, we were all distressed, shall we say you were not feeling quite the thing?" she said and went rambling on while her aunt, who had given up wondering and had given up listening and whose only feeling was of exhaustion as though she had been pounded for days, had enough strength left to know she had always disliked Claire, just as she had never got on with her mother.

When they were in that room upstairs where Julia had asked him not to muss her about, Amabel's first words were "kiss me" and this more than anything showed the difference between these two girls, not so much in temperament as in their relations with him.

After some time she drew back and powdered her nose. He walked round and round where she was sitting as though she were a river and a bridge off which he felt impelled to jump to drown.

"Be quiet," she said, "sit back."

He stood in front of her and she fixed him with her eyes which drew him like the glint a hundred feet beneath and called on him to throw himself over. He had always been drugged by heights and turned away experiencing that longing and demand to see again as they feel who want to jump when they look down. Her eyes were expressionless and brilliant.

"Darling," she said at last, "you didn't really mean to do that to me."

"I was mad."

"I thought you of all people couldn't mean it."

"I didn't."

"Didn't what?" she said, feeling her way.

"Mean it," he said.

They spoke slowly in soft voices and both of them now kept entirely still.

"When you rang up I knew it wasn't you speaking somehow, you sounded different. Why do we have to be like this to each other?"

"I'm the only one," he said, "I was mad."

"But why?"

"I don't know. Mad. Mad."

"Don't go on telling me you were mad," and here she raised her voice, "no one's mad these days! What was it?"

"This awful weather. Felt I had to get away," he mumbled.

"I'm sorry. But then what came between us to make you speak the way you did?"

"I don't know. I don't."

"And you knew what my doctor said, I told you. If you didn't want me to come you'd only to say so. That's been the wonderful thing about us."

"I did want you to."

"We've had that pact from the very beginning, if one of us wanted to go away you could or I could without saying a word. What made you ring up like that?"

"But I swear I wanted you to come."

"And then to lie to me like you did," she said, even softer. "To say just that you wouldn't come out to-night after you'd said you would. I'm not sure now what you did really say you upset me so."

"I was in an awful state," he said.

"Just when the doctor told me I ought to get away from this frightful weather and everything else. But all I want to do is understand. Darling, what made you do it?"

"I don't know."

"Well, we're both of us free, we can do as we want but what did make you do it?"

"Am, darling," he said, "don't you think you could come along," he said, not knowing her things were packed. "Do, darling, now, if it isn't too much. I always meant you to come."

"But, dear," she said, "what am I to believe? There's your voice over that beastly phone I wish it had never been invented, saying first that you would meet me to-night when you knew you were going and then again within twenty minutes saying you wouldn't be there."

"The first time I didn't know whether I was going or not."

"Didn't you? But then was it nice to invite me when you didn't know if you would turn up? Oh, Max, when you think of what our evenings have been."

"I know."

"I sometimes wonder if you ever have known at all."

"I'm hopeless."

"But why," she said, and pulled at her handkerchief, "if you would only tell me so I could understand."

There was a pause. She was looking over her shoulder away from him. He had been dazed but he hated tears, he never found them genuine and as he thought she might be going to cry he spoke more sharply, taking the initiative.

"Look, darling," he said, "it's this way. Come away with me now. Your maid can pack and follow on by aeroplane if she doesn't catch the train. Forget what I've been and let's have our lovely times over again. Darling, couldn't we?"

"What," she said, still looking away but not crying, "with all these other people, whoever they are?"

"Well, it's a bit awkward about them. We could leave them somewhere. It's really Evelyn Henderson. She's a very old friend and she's terribly badly off. I fixed it so they could all go for her really, whether I went or not."

She turned round, caught his eyes in the glare of hers and stamped.

"Don't you dare," she said and gasped. "Don't you, dare," she said in a small voice she was so angry, "try and put that over on me. It's Julia Wray and I've known it all along."

"Julia? What do you mean?"

"What do I mean? You are mad if you think I'll swallow that," and she laughed and spoke naturally. It was when she had herself under control that she could rule him.

"There's nothing about Julia.... I say..." he said and could not finish. He was under her command.

"Well, we had the arrangement," she said in her hard tone of voice, "we're both free," she was absolutely certain of him now, "we can both do as we like."

"Oh, no!"

"Yes, I know when I'm not wanted."

"You are. You're the point of the whole trip."

"You see I've come to know I can't trust a single thing you say. Max, my dear, you're hopeless and I don't know why I'm here. Try and think what you're saying."

"How d'you mean?"

"Don't play the innocent. The telephone."

"I tell you I was mad."

"But you weren't, you'd thought it out."

He began to think, to slip out of her control and be impatient. He showed it by not looking away when they met each other's eyes. As soon as she saw this she smiled at him. It was wonderfully done. She smiled in just the way she had done when first they became intimate, in such a way that she might have been talking to him almost under her breath when they had nothing, nothing between them.

He kissed her again. This time when she drew back she laughed.

"How much do you really want me to come?" she said.

He laughed.

"No, go on, how much, tell me, you must, how much," she said, as Julia had about her top. He looked at her, she was radiantly smiling, and again he felt lost and given over before her moods.

He went to kiss her again and she laughed and said no, no, not before he had told her.

"You know how much," he said and looked so expectant as to be idiotic.

"More than to go fishing," she said, calling on another afternoon.

"Yes."

"Even when the wind or whatever it was was just right."

"Of course."

"No," she said and looked at him as though he meant everything to her, "you remember, don't you, even if you had been waiting for whatever you have to wait for fishing even for weeks?"

"I do."

"Do you? No, you mustn't kiss me again, I haven't nearly finished. More than Ascot week, more than going to bed or staying up and, d'you remember, on that hill when you didn't want to go home?"

"Don't."

"Very well. What were we talking about before? Oh, blast you, why do you make me feel so sad?" she said and she made her eyes cloud over.

"Darling."

"All right, I'm not going to be tiresome or anything like that, but I can't think what I was doing when I fell for you," and she made way before him, making herself small.

"I do," he said, "because there's nobody like you."

"Isn't there?"

"Nobody like you."

"Is that all?" she said in her small voice. He laughed and kissed her again. This time she did not kiss him back but handed herself over.

When he found she had nothing on underneath she stopped him at once.

"No," she said, "hands off, I've just had my bath, I've just had my bath I tell you."

He got up and began walking round and round where she sat again. She had so wound him up that in his feeling for her as it was now he was thrown back on his grievance.

"What were you doing last night?" he said.

"How d'you mean?"

"When I rang up."

"Oh, then! Well, I did pop out for a moment," she said, looking long at her face in her glass.

"Who with?"

"We went to that cocktail club round the corner."

"Who's we?"

"No, let me finish," she said, putting more red on her lips. Her face blushed in spots where he had kissed her. "You've made such a mess of my face. Here, hold this," she said and gave him her mirror. His hand shook so he was no use to her. "Darling, you mustn't get upset about little things like that. It was only Richard and you know what he is."

"Embassy Richard?"

"Yes."

"Why him?"

"Why not, darling?"

"When I rang up you said Marjorie was with you."

"No, I didn't. You said you couldn't get on to me."

"I meant afterwards."

"Oh, then! I didn't want to tell you, that's all."

"It would take more than him to upset me," he said.

"Then what's the matter with you now?" she said sweetly.

"Nothing's the matter."

"I can't understand you these days at all. Here, give me back my mirror. What shall I do?" she said, "it is in a mess," tilting and turning her face from side to side.

"Well, what about it?"

"About Richard you mean? Why, nothing. By the way, he said he was coming on your train."

"You didn't invite him by any chance?"

"How could I? I'm not coming, you know, you didn't invite me. It's absurd, I can't just get packed like that at a moment's notice."

"Then I shan't go," he said, turning away and going back to the window.

She did not take much notice of this. "But, darling," she said, "you can't just leave them like that when you asked them."

"I can. I've given old Evelyn the tickets. It's arranged."

"But you can't, they're your guests. You mustn't be so independent. I won't let you. Think what they'll say."

"I don't care."

"Oh, yes, you do, you must care. The whole thing's absurd," and, forgetting she had just said she was not coming, "it's absurd," she said, "you say we can't go because Richard is in the hotel and travelling on the same train."

They did not either of them notice the slip she had made.

"How d'you know?" he said, turning round.

"I don't know," she said, looking at him, "only he said he would be here and when he says he will be somewhere, I believe him more than when you tell me the same thing."

"You've seen him?"

"Max, darling, don't be so ridiculous. I haven't set eyes on him since last night. He might be in Timbuctoo for all I care and anyway I don't know, darling. I must say, my dear, you don't seem very upset at my not coming."

"If you don't come, then I don't."

"Why must you be like this? I tell you you can't behave like that. You'll never be able to get anyone to go abroad with you again."

"I don't care." There was a pause. "In any case," he said, "I wasn't going to go."

"Then why did you say what you did when you rang me up the last time?"

"Because," he said, finding it at last, "because I saw with all this fog I might be with them for hours as the trains weren't running. I had to see them off, you know." He came up to her smiling.

"No, keep away," she said, "I've got to think this out." He's such an awful liar, she thought, but already everything seemed different. "No, I don't believe it," she said and began to hope.

"It's true," he said and then she knew he was lying and did not care. All she wanted from him was something reasonable like a password which would take her along without humiliation past frontiers and into that smiling country their journey together would open in their hearts as she hoped, the promised land. Not of marriage but of any kind of happiness, not for ever but while it lasted. She knew better than to want too much of any situation and marriage she had never wanted, though often imagined, after the first three weeks. It would have been better with almost anyone else but there it was, he fascinated her and so it was for her to fascinate him.

"Well then, supposing I did," she said.

"You really are going to come?"

"I might."

"That's good."

"Is that all you are going to say about it?"

"It's marvellous," he said. They kissed again. Some little time later it was he who drew away.

"Where's Embassy Richard going?"

She lay back irritated that he had left her.

"How should I know?"

"I suppose that party business was too much for him. London's getting too hot to hold him," he said.

"You know if I'm really going to go away with you you've got to be nice to me," she said.

"What d'you mean?"

"No tricks with the other girls, mind, or I'll be off home again."

"If you do," he said, "I'll go back with you."

"I shan't let you."

"I know more than to let you go off alone."

"That's being too silly for words," she said. "Why did you stop kissing me like that? And anyway, how many of those others have you kissed up here this afternoon?"

"Now it's you are being ridiculous."

"Not as I know you, my dear. Oh, well, go on then and kiss them. Who cares?"

"I don't kiss them."

"I suppose I'm being tiresome again, darling, am I? Never mind. Let's have a rest. No, don't kiss me again, please not, give my complexion a rest. Sit down here. I'll put my head on your shoulder and have a sleep." She yawned and settled herself down, shifted round a little, shut her eyes, breathed deeply twice and went off at once. She always could whenever she wanted.

As he sat there he realized he did not know if she was going to come or not. And if she did come out he did not know if she would stay or when she would get it into her head to start home which she might at any time. He realized without putting it into words he did not even know if he was glad she was going to come or sorry she was going to stay at home, he only knew that now she was here he would probably have to be with her wherever she made up her mind to be.

She lay on his shoulder in this ugly room, folded up with almost imperceptible breathing like seagulls settled on the water cock over gentle waves. Looking at her head and body, richer far than her rare fur coat, holding as he did to these skins which enfolded what ruled him, her arms and shoulders, everything, looking down on her face which ever since he had first seen it had been his library, his gallery, his palace, and his wooded fields he began at last to feel content and almost that he owned her.

Lying in his arms, her long eyelashes down along her cheeks, her hair tumbled and waved, her hands drifted to rest like white doves drowned on peat water, he marvelled again he should ever dream of leaving her who seemed to him then his reason for living as he made himself breathe with her breathing as he always did when she was in his arms to try and be more with her.

It was so luxurious he nodded, perhaps it was also what she had put on her hair, very likely it may have been her sleep reaching out over him, but anyway he felt so right he slipped into it too and dropped off on those outspread wings into her sleep with his, like two soft evenings meeting.

They slept and then a huge wild roar broke from the crowd outside. They were beginning to adjust that board indicating times of trains which had stood all of two hours behind where it had reached when first the fog came down. This woke him so that he started and this in turn woke her.

Like someone who is lost she did not know where she had been and in the same way neither of them knew how long they had been asleep so that when, after stretching and asking him where she might be, she found she was in this hotel she thought they had slept much longer than they had. She told him they must get down to join the others. She laughed. "They would never believe if we told them we had been asleep wrapped up in our clothes like babes in the wood," she said.

He wondered what it would be like to have Julia here in his arms to sleep on his shoulder for if he had only slept five minutes it was as though he had travelled miles. His sleep had made him forget the urgency of what Amabel had been.

"Yes," he said, "we've got to go."

"What's the hurry?" she said, noticing at once how he had changed, "they've waited all this time they can wait a bit longer."

But now he had become silent again and paid no attention to her. He smoothed down his clothes and straightened his tie while she lay back watching him. When he was done he came up to her politely smiling, took hold of her wrists and pulled her up. He did not kiss her, even when her coat fell open.

"There are times I hate you," she said.

Alex had been left alone again with Miss Crevy when Amabel had changed into her fur coat to lie in wait for Max to take him off upstairs. If all this delay had tried the crowd beneath he now found it intolerable and he suspected she was doing no more than bide her time until Max should come back to take a look at her again. He found that when Max was not there to look she lost interest and would hardly bother to answer him when he complained of how he felt. And when people paid no attention to his feelings this made him talk of these the more, so much so it was like a man whose hand trembles trying to pour red wine into a jug, he misses it and that wine falling on the table, shows red no more but is like water.

Pouring himself out as he did then, and faster because he was missing and more wildly he was so upset her jug was dry he got to such a pitch he stopped, humiliated, and wondered if she had even noticed, if he had even splashed some in. She gave no sign so that when Claire and Evelyn came back he began at once on them but this time he went further, he emptied all he had at once, and then more than he really had in mind. He tried to make Claire agree to give up the idea of going at any rate for today and, aiming better this time, went for her through her aunt.

"I must say, darling," he said, "I don't see very well how you can leave her even if she is much better as you say."

"I'm not the only one to say so," she explained, "Evelyn, you thought her ever so much better, didn't you, darling?"

"Really she's almost all right to look after herself. As a matter of fact" Evelyn said, and here she knew she was lying, "you said didn't you, darling, that you thought it silly of thinking to stay behind for her." Now Miss Henderson had never said this. It was true she had nearly said it. It was true she very much wanted to go today and that she was afraid if Claire had to stay that she would make her stay with her to have company when she was able to travel. You could make Robert Hignam do some things, he would carry messages, but they knew he would never stay behind because his wife had to. But Evelyn had never actually said it, at least she did not think she had because she had been too conscientious, too genuinely sorry for Miss Fellowes. Now Claire held the cup out for her to drink it was too much and she said "Yes, darling."

"Well, you know best," he said, "though I must say this, I'd think twice myself of leaving her to the tender mercies of those two old ghouls. And anyway, her companion or her nurse, or whatever she is, has fits, hasn't she?"

"My dear, what on earth has that to do with it?"

"Nothing I know. I remember calling on her once, I can't imagine why, and she practically had one on the doormat in front of me. I was just drawing a deep breath to scream for help when your aunt came out and whisked her away."

"How awkward for you," Miss Crevy said.

"Yes, wasn't it? But you see what I feel about all this is that it's too insane to stay here and the only thing to do is to go back home, unpack all over again and forget until to-morrow morning that we ever thought of going abroad to-day."

"But, good heavens!" Evelyna said, "what about the tickets?"

"Well, if Max wants us to come he can send us some more. We might just as well face it," he said, "we shall never see either of them again this evening, they're making whatever it is up upstairs and it will take hours. It's hopeless now, I know it is. And then half the suburbs are stranded down below. As things are now and with the government we have to-day, don't laugh, it's a serious thing, they are bound to evacuate them before they run our boat train."

"Alex," said Evelyn, "you're being absurd."

"But are you comfortable here?" he said, "have you ever in your life known such a frightful afternoon? We ought to be at Calais by now you know. And by the way, where's Julia?"

"She's upstairs with Max, isn't she?" said Miss Crevy.

"No," she said, "Amabel's with him."

"Well, couldn't they both be there?"

"Not possibly," he said.

"Well, all I know is Am went in there," she said, pointing to that bedroom door, "and I know she's still there."

"She went in to change into her fur coat and then they both went up. Evelyn and I saw them," said Claire. "I don't know where Julia can have got to."

"I don't care where anyone is," Alex said, "what I want is to go home."

"Then why don't you go?" Miss Crevy said.

"I can't, can I? Here are all you girls with no one to look after you, Robert is always in the bar; I can't possibly go," he said, and smiled, amused. "What would you do without me?"

"Really, Alex," Claire said, "you must be more careful. Why are you in such a state? And that's no reason for you to be rude."

"I'm sorry if I was, but don't you see there's no point in just one of us having enough and going off, we want to make a gesture and all go home and enjoy ourselves for a bit after the frightful time we've had."

Miss Crevy said: "You mean no one would miss you if you went alone."

"If you like, if you like," said he. "No, what I want is that we should make a demonstration."

"And what's the use of that?" Miss Henderson said, and turning out an enormous handbag she began counting over their tickets and reservations.

"You've got the tickets?" he said. "Why didn't you tell me? Why then the whole thing's simple, all we've got to do is to take them with us wherever we go to have a party, because we must have one to make up for all this, and make them come to us instead of waiting endlessly for them."

"I can't do it," said Claire. "I couldn't go away and leave my poor Auntie May."

"Really, Claire, that's fabulous," he said. "First you want to leave her behind when she's got no one but you and a maid who has fits, and then when it's a question of our all dropping her home you say you couldn't leave her."

"Alex, you're being impossible, darling."

"No, but why not do as I say and we'll all take her back."

"She's too ill to be moved," Miss Henderson said.

"Well, then leave her here then as you said at first. I take back what I said about those two old ghouls though they do sit like vultures round the dying—"

"Alex!"

"All right, I'm sorry—"

"No, Alex, it's not enough."

"All right—"

"Not enough to just say you're sorry every time."

"Well then," he said, raising his voice. "What do you want to do?"

"Where is Robert?" said Claire.

"What we want is," said Miss Crevy, "is for you to leave us alone."

"Even so you can't want to stay here."

"I don't know why not."

"Oh come on," he said to Claire, "it's a bad business all round, but don't let's suffer it in silence or in this sort of discomfort."

"I'm sorry, Alex, but I can't do anything."

"Evelyn," he said, about to appeal to Miss Henderson when Julia came in looking rather mad.

"My dears," she said panting, "they've broken in below, isn't it too awful?"

Alex laughed. "It would be too late," he said. Everyone else asked questions together.

"Why, all those people outside, of course," said Julia, "and they're all drunk, naturally. But what are we to do?"

"Who told you?"

"That man your Robert sent to find Thomson, Claire."

"Oh, my dear, I shouldn't believe anything he said."

"No, well he did seem rather odd about it and there you are. But what are we to do? Where's Max? Someone ought to tell him. Oh, what are we to do?"

"Now, Julia," Alex said, "there's nothing to get all worked up about—"

"No, darling, there really isn't," said Claire, and he went on:

"There's nothing to do, they won't come and kill us in our beds because we aren't in bed."

She turned away and stamped her foot at this, and Evelyn said: "Now, Alex—"

"No, seriously," he said, "they'll stay down by the bar if any have got in and they'll be got out of it in no time."

"Oh, but then they'll come up here and be dirty and violent," and she hung her handkerchief over her lips and spoke through it like she was talking into the next room through a curtain. "They'll probably try and kiss us or something."

"I'd like to see them try," said Miss Crevy.

"Now, Julia," Alex said, "you aren't in Marseilles or Singapore. You know an English crowd is the best behaved in the world. You'll be quite all right here."

She turned round. She was beside herself.

"Where's Max?" she said. "I must see him."

"And where's Robert?" Claire said, afraid for Julia.

"Max is upstairs with Amabel, darling."

"Oh no, Alex, how revolting," she said, and gave herself away. She blushed with rage. "You mean to say she's taken him upstairs just when this has happened."

"Oh, Julia my dear, do listen to me," Alex said. "Don't let it all run away with you."

"I don't know what you mean," she said, and became quiet with anger.

"It's this," he said, changing his ground. "Please don't think these people are violent or anything, because they aren't."

"And how d'you know?"

"Because they never are, they never have been in hundreds of years. Besides, if they have broken in as you say, well here we are inside and we can't hear a word. I mean, if they were breaking in down below we should hear shouts and everything. Robert would have come up to warn us. Really, you know, I don't think it can have happened. What I do say is it all proves we should never have stayed when we saw how bad this fog was." He spoke to them all. "That's all I've been getting at," he said, "and anyway it's obvious we can't get out now if we wanted to."

"Oh, why not?" said Julia.

"But, darling," Evelyn said, "for the very reason that all these people haven't got in, because it is all so locked up that not a soul can get in or out."

"Then how did that horrible man do it when Robert sent him to get hold of Thomson?"

"He's the house detective."

"No, he isn't," said Miss Crevy.

"And how d'you know?" he said.

"I don't," said she, "but there aren't any in this country."

"You go into a young man's room in any English hotel and you'll soon see."

"Don't be so personal, Alex. Really, what we've had to put up with from you this afternoon," Claire said, "and coming on top of everything else, it's too much."

"Look what we've all had to put up with," he said. "Oh, don't let's squabble."

"You mean to say," said Claire, "you don't think there's any chance of getting my Auntie May out of here any more? But then what's to happen to her if she has a turn for the worse? Oh, where is that idiotic Robert? Look here, Alex, I wonder if you would mind so terribly going down and bringing him back up here, you'll know where to find him, and he's simply got to do something about my aunt. Really, I've done enough, haven't I, Evelyn? Would you mind, Alex?"

"No," he said, "of course not, it's a good idea," and hurried out.

Claire began to explain him away to Miss Crevy. "I'm afraid you'll think him very odd, but he's had such a miserable time at home for so many years that we're all used to his being extraordinary so that doesn't surprise us a bit now, does it, darling?" she said to Julia to try and stop her thinking about herself. "Yes," she went on, "his mother died when he was ten and he was simply devoted to her," and here she began to speak like the older woman she was to become, "and then his father went mad and it took a long time or something, anyway it was absolutely exhausting whatever it was, and he has to go down and see him once every month wherever it is he's locked away. Then he has a sister that no one in the world has ever seen; she's got something the matter with her, too, and he's got very little money and he's perfectly marvellous about it, always paying out for them all the whole time, so that a trip like this means so much to him."

Miss Crevy was touched. "I didn't know," she said.

"Yes, so we all make rather special allowances for him," she went on, "don't we, darling?" she said to Julia. "It's all so miserable for him really, he hasn't had a chance."

"Why did we let him go? We'll never get him back."

"Now, Julia, do be a dear and don't fuss."

"But I am fussing. I'm fussing madly about my things. They'll run through my trunks and steal everything, and you know I can't travel without my charms."

"Well then my dear," said Evelyn Henderson, "what would you

like to do? Do you want to go or stay? You can't very well get out there and sit on your bags in all that crowd, and besides you would get so cold. Now settle down, darling, and wait till Alex comes back with Robert."

"Oh, I know," she said. "I know I'm being tiresome, but I can't help it, you see, things get too much for me, and it's so unfair of Max, who ought to be arranging everything for us, going away like this just when we want him most. That's why it suddenly seemed so fatal to let Alex go, we must have a man about in case those sorts of things happen."

"That's why I sent for Robert," said Claire. "I don't want to say anything behind his back that I wouldn't say to his face, but you know, Alex has been through so much and he's not one of those people who are made more useful by having had frightful things happen to them. In fact it always seems to me to have made him most frightfully selfish, as if after all those awful things he could only think of his own comfort."

"Yes, that's very true," said Evelyn.

"You know I think people so often go like that," Claire went on, "not that men are much use anyway, my God, no. Who is it has to get the cook out of the house when she's drunk, may I ask? But you have to have them around," she said to Julia, "but at the same time I don't count Alex as one of them, he's been through too much till somehow he's got nothing left."

Angela said it must have been rather awful for him, but perhaps he was one of those people who never had very much to start with.

"Oh, no," said Claire, too briskly, "he's a dear and a very great friend of mine. In many ways you can absolutely rely on him; no, I can't really have a word against Alex. I know he complains, but he never really bothers one if you get what I mean. He's not much use at a time like this, but then who would be with us stuck the way we are, and my aunt in the condition she's in. Evelyn, my dear, don't you think we ought to go back to see how she's getting on, though sometimes I feel as though we bring back luck with us every time we go into that room. What d'you say?"

"Shall I go?" said Evelyn.

"Oh no, darling, I can't leave you to do all my duties. It's sweet of you," she said, and they went out together.

Julia thought how selfish everyone is, they go on bothering about their aunts and don't give one thought to how others are feeling. They were all the same, but Max was the worst, it was too low to be making love upstairs in the same room he had tried to pounce on her when they all wanted him and when there were thousands of things waiting which only he could settle. At this Miss Crevy, whom Julia was always forgetting as though she did not properly exist, spoke up and said:

"Would you like me to come down with you to see if we can do anything about your things?"

This seemed to Julia the sweetest thing she had ever heard, to offer to brave those frantic drinking hordes of awful people all because someone was upset about their charms and all the more because this angelic angel could not know about them or what they meant to her or about her and how miserable she got. She was made better at once for, like delicate plants must be watered every so often so Julia must have sympathy every now and then, as Alex must have someone to listen to him, and once she had it was all right for another little while. So Julia refused but so warmly Miss Crevy was surprised into thinking she could only be engaged to Max who, she now realized, must be upstairs with Amabel.

It was at this moment that Max came in with Amabel, so that Julia knew she would almost at once forget about her charms now he was back, and all her worries.

When he was in the room she could even stand apart and watch herself, she grew so confident. She thought he looked terrific, but when she had taken in Amabel's new looks and her brilliant eyes, she thought she was most like a cat that has just had its mouse coming among other cats who had only had the smell.

He was why she changed so she would forget what she had been six minutes back, he it was who nagged at her feelings when he was not there, and when he came in again worked her up so she had soon to go out though not for long, it was his fault, but then she knew it to be hers for being like she was about him, oh, who would be this kind of a girl, she thought.

Before anyone had spoken the telephone rang and while Max said "what's this," and went to answer it, Amabel arranged herself where she had been sitting before.

"Yes," he said into it, "yes, she's here. No, shall I take a message?" and he turned to look at Julia, so that she knew they were ringing her up. She went across to be at hand. "You mean now?" he asked. "I see. You understand this is my party, mind," he said, "it is Mr. Adey speaking. Yes, we'll be ready," and he rang off.

He put his arm through Julia's and pressed his elbow tight against it and this to her was as though he knew everything and that he was sorry for anything he might have done and that anyway it was all right. It was like sugar and water fed to plants in a last emergency and was what she had been ordered. "Well," he said, as though it was as easy as anything, "we've got to get ready to go, they've just rung me up."

I can't bear it, Julia said to herself, it's too wonderful, it's too much. If we go now everything will come right, but if only we go now this instant minute, it must be at once, oh, please.

Angela said "goody" and Julia thought of a difficulty. "But how on earth?" she cried and he said gently, "by the lift." Amabel sat on as though she had not heard as people do who know it will all be the same wherever they may be and who have maids to look after them.

"Oh, you don't understand," said Julia off her balance and wildly excited, "you can't, no one can go, they've broken in below you see, d'you mean they really want us to be off?"

"I say," Angela said, "my luggage is in the cloakroom."

Max said he would see to that and Julia began. She rambled, not pronouncing what she was saying very well and looking sideways at the carpet while she now pressed his arm hard with hers. She wanted to know what she was to do about Thomson and when their train would go, did she have time to get ready, and again how would they get out as Max had not heard about the crowds that had broken in and hadn't they better ring her uncle up to find out if it was safe? Max took no notice of her except he said once he would look after it and gradually Julia began to run down and as she did so happiness came back to her, budding out of her fingers and her cheeks and hair like new landscapes open with a change of season after frost. She felt she was living again and with that feeling she wondered if she had not been rather ridiculous perhaps. She said Evelyn and Claire ought to be told and with that she suddenly left them and ran out, and looking back in through the door she said, "but we haven't to go just at once, have we?" and then was gone again.

Radiantly happy she rushed into that room Miss Fellowes lay in and thinking that she would be unconscious, burst out saying, "children we are to go, they've telephoned to say it's all over, isn't it wonderful and we're to get ready, darlings, just think."

But Miss Fellowes, who was sitting up in bed, took this to mean that they were at last ready to remove her.

"My dear," she said, "I'm very glad to hear it, I feel I've been here long enough, though Claire will insist on saying I ought to stay the night."

Julia had not seen Miss Fellowes when she came in so that it was a shock to hear her voice and more than a shock to see her propped up in bed exhausted. She looked as if she had been travelling.

Julia had never thought of her as being old. She had been brought up with Claire and so had always known Miss Fellowes who had in consequence seemed ageless to her in that her appearance had not altered much in all those years. And now she saw her all at once as very old and for the last time that day she heard the authentic threatening knock of doom she listened for so much when things were not going right. But it was impossible for anything to upset her now they were really going.

"Why, Auntie Fellowes," she said, "I never saw you and there you are sitting up in bed. Why you see," she rushed on, "it's for us, our train is going to run after all, isn't it wonderful?"

"Darling," said Claire, "I was telling Auntie May she really must be good and stay here for a while, at least until she gets her strength."

"But I feel quite well now, Claire, quite well."

"You must be careful, darling, really."

"Now, darling Aunt Fellowes," Julia said, "you mustn't get in a fuss."

She was about to say she was in no fuss and that all she asked, and it was reasonable enough, was to be allowed to get better in the comforts of her home, when she realized it would be better to let them think they were having their own way like Daisy had when they put her in that asylum. She had kept on telling them how glad she was to be there until they had pronounced her sane and let her go. She could remember now Daisy saying they would have put her in the strait-jacket if she had resisted, so she determined to say nothing but unfortunately she was so weak she began to cry. She began to shake also. Claire kissed her and said she was to rest and not to worry and took those other two girls out with her again.

They stood outside in the corridor and Julia, who was unaffected, she was so excited at their going away, said she was sorry, she had no idea she would be able to hear anything, she had thought she would still be unconscious.

"Well, it was rather a pity, darling," Claire said, "and just when I was telling her we could not move her out or get her doctor in."

"She's ill," Julia said, "and she'll just have to get used to the idea. When one's ill one's ill and there's an end of it, one has to stay there till one gets better."

"I was thinking," Claire said, "you know I don't think I can come, not now anyway, I can't leave her like that. I'd never forgive myself if anything happened to her."

"Darling, you can't speak like that," said Julia quite serene. "If you don't come then I won't either, I couldn't go without you when our party's in the state it's in." She spoke gaily, certain that Claire did not mean what she said.

"But, my dear, Max would never forgive me if I was the cause of your not going just because I had an aunt who was taken ill on the platform. My dear, he'd never speak to me again. She's been enough nuisance to him already, you can't mean to say you'd let her break the whole thing up."

"Well, if you don't go, I won't."

"But look, I shall be coming on in a few days, to-morrow probably."

"No, Claire my dear, no Claire no Julia. Besides," she said, more serious, "you know what the doctor said, there's nothing really the matter with her, is there? Why don't you let her go home if that is what she really wants?"

"Why here's that idiotic Robert," Claire said. As he came up to them foolishly smiling, she said:

"Have you been drinking?"

"Yes."

"Are you drunk?"

"No, of course I'm not."

"There's no of course about it as I know you," she said, examining him.

Julia explained. "It's too awful, Robert dear," she said. "I've gone and upset your aunt. You see the great news is that we've been told to get ready to go at last and I rushed into her room and told them and she thought it was meant for her and was so disappointed when Claire told her she couldn't be moved yet, poor darling," she said cheerfully.

"What are we to do about her?" Claire said to Robert.

"I don't know."

"Then why don't you know?" Claire was always much harder on him when others were present. When they were alone she was another person and knowing this made her easier for him to bear.

"She's not my aunt," he said and laughed.

"She is, aren't we married? Oh, now my darlings, you see what I have to put up with."

"Well, what do you want to do?" he said shrewdly.

"You wouldn't think it very awful if I left her now, would you?" Claire began. "You see she has Nanny and her friend to look after her and she does seem so much better at last. Of course she is awfully weak and it was rather naughty of Julia to come in like that and upset her, but really when all's said and done I think she is getting to the age," Miss Fellowes was fifty-one, "when it's better for them to do what they want when they are ill. D'you remember what the doctor said when your father died, but of course she's not as bad as that, only she does worry me so, I'm afraid she's not so well really. Robert, think now, what d'you say about it? You don't think it would be very awful of me, really?"

"Of course not," he said and he had only been waiting to agree with whatever it was she wanted. "Of course not," he said.

Now it was settled they should go and that Claire would come with them in spite of Miss Fellowes, Julia went back to Max expecting to find them getting ready. Amabel had gone to dress but those others had opened the windows and were leaning out. She went behind Max and said, "Don't move, it's me," and willed her leg where it touched his to tell him she was glad.

Looking down they could see which platforms had already been opened, for at the gates a thin line of people were being extruded through in twos and threes to spread out on those emptier platforms. Separated there they became people again and were no longer menaces as they had been in one mass when singing or all of their faces turning one way to a laugh or a scream. She could even smile at them, they were so like sheep herded to be fold-driven, for they were safe now, they could be shepherded into pens and journey back to food, home, warmth and sleep. Again, if they had broken in below, which she was ready now to disbelieve, they would slowly begin to drain away again, their tide had turned and when they raised one last cheer as the first train went out she swallowed she was so afraid she was going to cry. Dear good English people, she thought, who never make trouble no matter how bad it is, come what may no matter.

Max turned away when he had seen enough, and probably because she had given up watching and had been looking at the back of his head and had been loving him, so because she had been feeling for him when he should have been loving her without her having to do one thing about it, then she began to try and worry at him again.

"Well," she said, "here we all are, why don't we go?"

"Am's not ready yet," he said.

"Then hadn't you better tell her to hurry up. They won't keep our train back for us while we dress, you know." He said they had told him there was not that much hurry and put his arm through Julia's once more.

"But how," she said, "how on earth when we do go do we get through all those people there are still down there, can you tell me that?"

"They said they would take us along this floor through the hotel and then the office till we can get down by a lift on to the place they keep for visiting big noises, where they receive them you see."

"Oh, Max, as though they held receptions for noises," she said, but he did not laugh, he never laughed at himself. Besides he had just surprised himself regretting that Amabel was coming with them.

When she had first come in it was guilt had made him so worked up about her but this feeling had gone when he saw how she was working on him until he had begun to feel his influence over her and had become indifferent, so that he did not care if she went or stayed. Finally, back to Julia as he was now and with Angela Crevy in reserve he would much rather Amabel stayed behind. Besides there was Embassy Richard. He could not stand him.

"Where's Embassy Richard?" he said. "Has anyone seen the man?"

They all exclaimed at this and Alex, who had come back when he found Robert Hignam, turned round from his window where he had been leaning out.

"Richard?" he said, "where?"

"Someone said so. I haven't seen him."

"Why then," said Alex, "we can ask him straight out if he did write that letter."

"And d'you suppose he'd really tell you?" said Miss Crevy.

"No, I know," he said because he now wanted to be amiable, he thought he had gone rather far before, "I suppose he wouldn't."

And so everything now hung on Amabel, as it had done earlier when she was not there for even then she had remote control over Max so that she might have been some sort of a Queen Bee. At first he had hidden himself from them because he could not but feel guilty about her and then when they had found him he had still been hiding; his fun such as it was at that time had been stolen as he had known she would find him out. Now that she had found him he wanted fun and no longer cared how he got it, but one cannot break into houses when in the station cell and she had the key. So he wondered if he could get Richard to come along with them to keep her occupied. And now she came back in again.

"Where is he?" he said. "I'd better find him," and he left Julia to telephone.

"But, darling," she said, following, "I thought you hated him."

"No, good chap, Richard."

He made enquiries and was told which room he was in. He asked to be put through.

"What on earth are you up to now?" Amabel said, and Julia knew at once by her voice there had been trouble. She moved away from him slightly, hoping they would have a row and so as not to distract his attention from how tiresome she hoped Amabel would be.

"I'm going to get him along."

"But have you thought at all? I mean does anyone want him?" she said.

"Oh, rather, lots of questions for him, ask Alex."

"Is that you, Richard?" he said, "I say, come along and have a drink. Come on," and he gave their room number.

"You aren't really going to ask him about that letter are you?" Miss Crevy said to Alex. "It may embarrass him terribly, you know."

"It may," Alex said, "but he'd rather we did, I think."

"But it's not something to be proud of, is it? I'd have said he would hate it. Isn't it rather hitting a man when he's down?" and she said this in such a way, stressing the word "man," that made it sound as though everyone kicked, bit, and hit women when they were down.

"Oh, I agree with you, it is," Alex said, "but you see he'll enjoy it, he'd be sorry if we didn't, but if you like we won't say anything, we'll let him start it on his own. He enjoys it you see. I'll bet you he'll bring it up himself within five minutes."

"Then I think it's revolting."

"Darling," Julia said to her, still hoping Max and Amabel would quarrel about him, "it's because like when one is shy about something one simply can't stop talking about it. And besides he wants everyone he meets to tell him it's all right."

"Well," Max said to Amabel, as though she had been speaking for Angela Crevy, "here he is now, we'll see," and at that he came in.

Mr. Richard Cumberland was not unlike Alex and when he spoke his manner was much the same. He said, "Why, hullo, my old dears," and shook hands all round. If he could he took each hand in one of his, if only one was offered, then he took hold with both hands. He did not shake, he pressed as though to make secrets he would never keep, as though to embrace each private thought you had and to let you know he shared it with you and would share it again with anyone he met. As against this, when he spoke it was never to less than three people. It may have been tact, or that he was circumspect, but he paid no attention to Amabel.

"You've all heard about my little bit of trouble," he said, "well the town's too hot to hold me now. You know I put that thing in all the papers about my not being able to come to something or other, well they all made such a fuss you'd never believe so I thought it was time for little Richard to say good-bye for now and here I am."

"What a pity," Alex said, "what a pity."

"You don't sound very glad all of you to see me."

"My dear, I couldn't be more pleased in every way, you must know that, only we had such arguments about who did send that announcement to the papers and I said all through it had been you so..."

"Oh no Alex, excuse me you never did," Miss Crevy said, "just the opposite really, you know. You always said someone else had sent it."

"There you are," Alex said to him, "it's been like this the whole time and there you've been not three minutes away, my dear, and we never know."

"I say, Richard," said Max, "where are you aiming for?"

"Why?" he said, smiling round at all of them.

"Why don't you come with us?"

"D'you all really mean it?" he said, "well, yes, I might."

"That's fixed then," said Max and fixed it was.

So for anything in the world, it seemed to Julia, it was most like that afternoon when Miss Fellowes had said let's take the child to a matinee, when she had never yet gone to the theatre, it was so wonderful to see Max planning as he must be doing, to keep Amabel occupied with someone for herself. So like when you were small and they brought children over to play with you and you wanted to play on your own then someone, as they hardly ever did, came along and took them off so you could do what you wanted. And as she hoped this party would be, if she could get a hold of Max, it would be as though she could take him back into her life from where it had started and show it to him for them to share in a much more exciting thing of their own, artichokes, pigeons and all, she thought and laughed aloud.

"But weren't you going anywhere?" Amabel said to Richard, only she looked at Max.

"I can go where I was going afterwards," he said to all of them and smiled.

London,
1931–1938

OTHER NEW YORK REVIEW CLASSICS

For a complete list of titles, visit www.nyrb.com or write to:
Catalog Requests, NYRB, 435 Hudson Street, New York, NY 10014